"You know perfectly well why I married you."

Sally spoke in a crisp voice. "After all, you spelled it out for me yourself."

Paul's smile became detectably cynical. "The talented brother and the needy grandparent. Sally the family sacrifice," he mocked.

She didn't like that. It made her sound like a wimp. "Not at all. I made a bargain, just as you did."

"How fortunate that I could meet your price." The smooth voice held a hard edge.

"Take that back!" she said furiously. "I won't be talked to like some tawdry gold digger."

Paul tipped his head back, and his eyes flickered. "Why not? Don't like the truth, Sally?"

Sophie Weston wrote and illustrated her first book at the age of five. After university she decided on a career in international finance, which was tremendously stimulating and demanding, but it was not enough. Something was missing in her life, and that something turned out to be writing. These days her life is complete. She loves exciting travel and adventures, yet hates to stray too long from her homey cottage in Chelsea, where she writes.

Books by Sophie Weston

HARLEQUIN ROMANCE

HARLEQUIN PRESENTS

Don't miss any of our special offers. Write to us at the following address for information on our newest releases.

Harlequin Reader Service
P.O. Box 1397, Buffalo, NY 14240
Canadian address: P.O. Box 603,
Fort Erie, Ont. L2A 5X3

HABIT OF
COMMAND
Sophie Weston

Harlequin Books

TORONTO • NEW YORK • LONDON
AMSTERDAM • PARIS • SYDNEY • HAMBURG
STOCKHOLM • ATHENS • TOKYO • MILAN
MADRID • WARSAW • BUDAPEST • AUCKLAND

Original hardcover edition published in 1992
by Mills & Boon Limited

ISBN 0-373-03274-9

Harlequin Romance first edition July 1993

HABIT OF COMMAND

Printed in U.S.A.

CHAPTER ONE

LOUD noises came from the inner office. Sally Harrison, trying to ignore them, typed hard at the keyboard.

She dropped her dark head over the computer, feeling harassed. She had promised to be home by seven-thirty tonight. There was a Parent Teacher Association meeting and she had promised Andrew that she would go.

But the way Paul Theokaris and his uncle were shouting at each other behind the large oak door filled her with foreboding that she would, yet again, have to break her promise.

'I will not,' Costas Theokaris was roaring.

Paul's voice, answering him, was a low rumble. Paul, as Sally had learned over the last four years as his personal secretary, very seldom raised his voice. In spite of that, and his spectacular dark good looks, he was much more widely feared than his uncle. When the job fell vacant, it had not been an easy task to find a girl willing to work for him.

'Crazy!' Costas declared.

Sally read through the contract she had just finished typing. Then she pressed a button and printed it off. She stood up, stretching, while the printer creaked into life. She was stiff and very tired but Paul had said he wanted to see the contract tonight. Even so, he would not welcome her intruding on his fight with Costas. That was another thing Sally had learned early in the job: family was taboo.

She sighed. Paul had, unusually, raised his voice in reply and his words were all too plain.

'I won't be blackmailed. If that's what you want then you can have my resignation now. The whole damn family can have it.'

Costas, who had spent his youth as captain of his own ship and never ceased to regret his promotion to a shore job, gave a bellow that would have reached from one end of an oil tanker to the other.

'Don't take that tone with me. The family will kick you out...'

'Right.' It was no more than a snarl but it penetrated the walls in a way that made Sally take several steps backwards and look apprehensively at the door. It was not unknown for the Theokaris family to throw furniture when they were in a passion. 'You can have my resignation now. I never wanted the job in the first place...'

And that, Sally thought, collecting her papers from the printer, was only too true. Until his father had had that heart attack Paul Theokaris had never come near the family or its various businesses.

In fact he had been a more than successful businessman in his own right. The management consultancy firm he had built up from scratch had been a European market leader when he was recalled to take charge of the floundering Theokaris empire.

It was in the consultancy that Sally had first worked for him. She had been a little surprised when he took her with him when he had moved. But he had answered her unasked question by saying darkly that he wanted at least one person working for him in the Theokaris Corporation who knew what she was doing.

'Don't think you can get away with anything you fancy here,' Costas was shouting now. 'You're responsible to a board now——'

'I am indeed,' Paul interrupted. He sounded silky. 'A board who begged me on their knees to dig them out of the hole you'd got them into.'

This was a low blow. He must be very angry, Sally thought, to throw that at his uncle.

She could hear his voice softening, as if he regretted it already. 'Don't be a fool, Costas. I'll do my duty but, by heaven, I won't sell my soul. The company can survive without human sacrifice.'

There was a roar at this pronouncement that shook the walls and set the papers on Sally's desk fluttering. The door was flung violently back on its hinges.

'No,' said Paul Theokaris with finality.

Costas shot out of the room and past Sally's desk with a face of thunder.

She looked down at the papers she held. When she looked up Paul was standing in the doorway, one hand braced against its frame, looking after his uncle with a black expression. He seemed completely unaware of Sally, she thought wryly.

'Er—do you still want to look at this contract to-night?' she murmured.

He flashed her a look in which impatience and irritation were nicely balanced.

'Want to get home, do you?' he said.

In normal circumstances Paul Theokaris could not, by any stretch of the imagination, be called a considerate boss. Now he sounded positively thunderous. Sally met his accusing eyes calmly. She worked well and long hours, as they both knew. Paul also knew that it would be difficult to find another secretary who was willing to work evenings and weekends at the flick of his fingers; or at least not unless she had a crush on him. And, as they also both knew, Sally did not fall into that category.

So she did not say anything to defend herself and, after a second, Paul stopped glaring at her and left his post in the doorway. He came and stood by her desk, holding out a hand for the papers. His other hand ran absently through his dark curls.

He looked preoccupied and, Sally thought with compassion, tired. She said gently, 'I ought to go. I should catch the six-twenty. I promised. I told you.'

He did not answer. She sighed.

'I suppose I could ring home.'

Paul looked up at that, quickly. In spite of the underlying weariness, he gave her that smile of flashing charm. It was the reason that Sally's three predecessors had originally thought working for Paul Theokaris was the most wonderful job in the world, notwithstanding the antisocial hours. It was the reason also that Paul Theokaris had, when it came to his attention, eased each one of the three out of his office and given the personnel director instructions that he wanted his next secretary to be a domestically satisfied wife and mother.

Sally did not quite fit the description. Paul had only accepted her candidature, she thought drily, after he'd met her and seen for himself that her devotion to her family was quite as great as that of any mother. She and her brother were orphans who had been brought up by an elderly grandfather, who was now, Paul understood, infirm and hard-up. Andrew, the brother for whom she was responsible, was fifteen.

Now he sighed. 'I know. I forgot. I'm sorry, Sally. Why do you put up with me?'

'The money,' Sally said cheerfully.

Paul made a face. 'Yes, I suppose I'm lucky the company can afford to pay over the odds,' he said with unwonted bitterness. 'Or I'd never get a secretary at all.'

Sally took the papers out of his hands, shuffled them into an orderly pile, and put them into a neat folder.

She took them across to the safe, dialled the combination, swung it open and stowed the contract away.

'You'd find a way,' she said drily, swinging the reinforced door shut and twirling the dial.

He watched her, still a little grim. When he next spoke he startled her.

'You don't think much of me, do you, Sally?'

With a quick glance at her watch she logged off from her work station. Paul watched her with a curious expression.

'Do you?' he persisted.

She picked up her shoulder-bag and turned to face him.

'What's brought this on? You're not normally introspective at this hour of the evening.'

He said slowly, 'I want to know.'

She shook her head. 'Don't be silly. Look, I'm late——'

'I'll drive you home,' he said swiftly.

It was not the first time he had done so. But he did not normally offer on the spur of the moment like that and certainly not at an hour when she could perfectly well still catch a commuter train.

Sighing, Sally put down her bag and sat behind her desk. She picked up the telephone and pressed the button that activated the system's automatic dialling of her home number.

Andrew answered.

'Andy? Look, honey, something's come up. I'll probably go straight to school. How late can I afford to be?'

Andrew, predictably, was unconcerned.

'You don't really need to go at all,' he assured her with the earnestness of a boy whose last report had been dotted with 'could do better's and 'must try harder's.

'Oh, yes, I do,' said Sally. 'You and Gramps go on. Tell Miss Firmin I'll be there as soon as I can.'

Andrew sighed. 'OK.'

She put the phone down. Paul Theokaris bent forward, putting both hands on either edge of her desk. He looked at her searchingly.

'You take your responsibilities seriously.'

Sally met his eyes with composure.

'Of course,' she said.

He straightened. 'Get your coat.'

She sighed. He had a rich man's car, sleek and fast and upholstered in cream leather. The speed at which he drove frightened her and even so he would only get her home ten minutes quicker than the train. She had never had the heart to tell him.

'There's no need,' she said without much hope.

But Paul was already talking to the garage on her telephone. There was no way of avoiding his determined goodwill. Sally pulled on her jacket and knotted the bright scarf round her throat.

Paul put down the telephone and looked her over appraisingly.

'Smart,' he said with a faintly surprised note in his voice.

'Thank you,' Sally said, unmoved.

Paul Theokaris did not normally comment on her clothes. However, his Paris-dressed female family, to say nothing of a string of elegant girlfriends, well qualified him to pass an opinion.

He grinned suddenly. 'Impervious to all compliments, Sally? Or just mine?'

She laughed. 'Well, since that's part of the job description, I'm surprised you need to ask.'

Paul looked taken aback. 'As bad as that?'

'"He's a great charmer. Don't believe a word he says. If you do, he'll chuck you out".' She reported the personnel officer's advice with a glint.

'Good lord,' Paul said blankly. He held the door open for her. 'No wonder——' He stopped.

'No wonder what?' Sally prompted as she passed.

He closed the door gently, put a hand under her elbow and led her along the softly carpeted corridor to the lifts. At this time of night there was no one about on the management floor.

'No wonder what?' she insisted as the lift doors closed on them.

Paul gave her an odd look, as if he were calculating the reaction of a business opponent.

But all he said was, 'Never mind.'

The car was warm from its sojourn in the garage. Costas had used it to return from a luncheon engagement at the Savoy and the interior was redolent of Havana cigar and faint heady alcohol fumes. Sally's nose twisted distastefully.

Seeing her expression, Paul said in amusement, 'You don't really approve of my executive toys either, do you?'

Sally tucked her long legs in front of her and shrugged. He went round to the other door, swung himself inside and nodded to the garage attendant as he gunned the engine.

'At least it will get you home faster than British Rail,' he said with a slight edge to his voice.

He drove fast even in the crowded City streets. Sally sat beside him with her hands clasped on her bag, trying not to let her nervousness show. She had trained herself not to press her foot against the floorboards when she thought that he should brake—a view that he hardly ever shared.

Paul sent her a quick glance under his eyelids but he did not comment on that tension. In fact, he did not say

anything at all until they were south of the river and
cruising on a dual carriageway.

'My uncle Costas has been giving me some advice,'
he said. It sounded as if he was musing aloud.

'Your uncle Costas wouldn't give you the time of day
if he thought he could get a dollar for it,' Sally muttered.

She was tired and edgy or she would not have allowed
herself that indiscretion. Normally she did not offer any
views on the various members of the Theokaris family
with whose demands Paul had to deal. Her private
opinion was that he was more patient and generous than
the clan deserved. But he did not confide in her and she
did not offer gratuitous familiarities.

So now there was considerable astonishment in the
look he shot her; astonishment and something else, Sally
thought uneasily. It was that calculating, negotiating look
again. There was a pause.

'He thinks I ought to marry. A nice girl,' Paul said
airily.

Sally sniffed. 'My sympathies are with the nice girl,'
she told him.

Paul did not seem to be offended.

'I'm inclined to agree with you,' he murmured. 'So
what do you suggest?'

'Me?'

Sally turned her head to stare at him. He had never
made any such remark to her before. She let her eyes
drift down to the speed gauge. Yes, he was driving fast,
but not *insanely* fast. Perhaps he had not lost his wits.

'You know me pretty well.' He sounded amused.
'What do you think I should have in a wife?'

They were coming to a fork in the road at which they
needed to filter right. Paul did it without checking his
speed. Sally's heart lurched.

'An armour-plated Amazon,' she snapped.

He gave a soft laugh. 'Just the lines I was thinking along myself,' he agreed.

But after that the road became too convoluted, and Sally had to concentrate too hard on reminding him of the route for the conversation to continue.

They drew up outside the terraced house with less than Paul's usual panache. In fact he had to manoeuvre to slot his sleek Jaguar in between an old Ford and a battered van bearing an advertisement for a double-glazing firm. Sally sighed. She had lived in the house ever since her parents had died, and it was home. But there were times when she wished it looked a little less shabby.

Paul, who inhabited an interior-designed apartment in Knightsbridge, did not spare the peeling paint so much as a glance. Instead, and most uncharacteristically, he sat there, drumming his fingers' ends on the wheel.

Sally made to open the door.

'Thank you,' she said formally. 'It was kind of you...'

He made an impatient gesture. Whatever else you could say of Paul Theokaris, Sally thought, and she said a lot in the privacy of her home, you could not say he had any illusions about his own character.

He said, 'Can I come in for coffee?'

Sally stared in undisguised astonishment. Her mouth curled in an involuntary grin. He sounded for all the world like one of the nervous boyfriends she had had in her teens.

'What are you laughing at?' he demanded disagreeably.

Sally composed her face. 'Nothing,' she assured him.

He gave her a narrow-eyed look but did not press her. Perhaps, she thought, he realised he would not like the answer. She folded her lips to prevent herself chuckling again.

'Well?' It was a challenge.

Sally sighed. She looked at her watch. Neither Andrew nor her grandfather was waiting anxiously at the front-room window. It was possible, of course, that they had followed her instructions and gone ahead to the school. Possible but unlikely. She had very little doubt that they were tucked comfortably in front of the television, even though Grandfather's sight was too bad for him to be able to see it properly, hoping that she would be too late for the PTA meeting. They would greet Paul's advent rapturously.

'Oh, very well,' she said. 'But you can't stay long. I've got to go to my brother's school.'

'Ah, yes, the substitute son,' Paul murmured as he got out of the car.

He opened the passenger door for her and stood there smiling down at her as if he were his own chauffeur, she thought as icy rage welled up. She had been accused of being too possessive of Andrew before and it never failed to reduce her to fury.

'I beg your pardon?' she said, not moving.

Paul looked surprised. 'The next best thing to a husband and children,' he reminded her. 'My insurance policy that you won't set out to entrap me.'

Slowly Sally got out. She had long, graceful legs and knew it. She ignored his outstretched hand but she was aware of his admiring glance and was secretly pleased.

'I would not,' she assured him sweetly, 'seek to entrap you even without that insurance policy. Believe me, I see quite as much of you as my blood-pressure will tolerate as it is.'

Paul shook his head but his eyes glinted.

'Very sensible. If a little unkind.'

Sally extracted her front-door key. She did not dignify this mischievous remark with a reply. They walked up the untidy path side by side. The crocuses, she noticed for the first time, had died off and ought to be deadheaded. There was never enough time to deal with even their tiny patch of garden. If it had been anyone but Paul Theokaris at her side—her auntie Mary, say—she would have pointed it out and apologised. But she was not in the business of apologising to Paul.

To her surprise he twitched the key from her hand and opened the front door. As if, she thought, it were the door to the sort of penthouse where he was no doubt used to taking coffee with young women.

'Thank you,' she said drily, retrieving her keys and storing them carefully in her handbag. She was not good with keys.

Paul chuckled. 'Why do I have the feeling I'm not your ideal visitor? Or is it just local custom? In Greece you would say "My house is your house".'

She raised her eyebrows. He had a habit of presenting her with snippets of information about his native customs. Sally was darkly suspicious of the information, most of which sounded pure fairy story. She was quite clear, however, that its objective was to get Paul something he wanted and did not otherwise envisage achieving. Since he had more than once successfully fished for an invitation to stay to supper when he drove her home, she concluded that that was probably what he wanted now.

'In Greece,' Sally said carefully, 'I doubt if any self-respecting unmarried girl would let you over her threshold. And you can stop looking wounded. I'm not feeding you tonight, no matter how tired and lonely you are. I'm going to Andrew's PTA meeting if it kills me.'

Paul chuckled, not replying. He followed her into the shadowed hall. It was narrow and dark. Sally had done what she could with ivory paint but there was no disguising its shabbiness. The stair carpet was threadbare and the coats hanging on the wall-hooks were scuffed and out at elbow. Seeing them with Paul's eyes, Sally felt suddenly acutely protective of her home and family.

'Come through into the sitting-room,' she said with a touch of sharpness. 'I'll put the kettle on.'

The sound of the television was plain. Two faces, expressions between guilt and defiance, looked up as they went in. Andrew jumped up, but Grandfather sat where he was with resolution.

'Got home quick,' he said, the clouded eyes still managing to snap under his bushy grey eyebrows. 'Evening, young man.'

Sally sighed again. Her grandfather had brought her up to believe that all men were created equal. While she agreed with him wholeheartedly, sometimes she wished he would refrain from giving expression to his democratic principles by addressing her employer like that. Still, 'young man' was better than 'lad', which was what he habitually called Paul if he spoke to him on the telephone.

Paul, to be fair, had met him on a number of occasions, in this house and elsewhere, and never gave any sign of being offended.

Now he said absently, 'Good evening, Mr Harrison.'

Andrew switched off the television and ran his fingers through his hair. It had plainly not seen a comb since she had sent him off to school that morning, Sally thought. Grandfather was no friend to what he called 'all that washing and brushing up'.

'Hello, Mr Theokaris,' Andrew said shyly.

Unlike Gramps, he was impressed by Paul Theokaris. One look at the Jaguar and Andrew had been positive that, no matter how late Sally had to work or how early she got him up in the morning to have breakfast before she left, she was working for absolutely the right guy.

'Coffee,' Sally said briskly. Andrew behaving beautifully was a fearsome sight. 'Do you want some?'

Grandfather would have tea. Andrew would help make the coffee. He followed her out into the kitchen as Paul, at her grandfather's invitation, sank on to the old sofa and gave his opinion on Millwall's chances in the Cup.

'What's he doing here?' hissed Andrew, clattering mugs and a jar of instant coffee.

'He brought me home,' Sally said repressively, although she was wondering very much the same thing herself.

Andrew, who liked his coffee strong, ladled a couple of spoonfuls of instant coffee into every mug. Sally removed half the granules from each.

'You didn't say he was coming.'

'I didn't know.'

'Why has he?'

Sally stared at him. 'Do you know, I'm not quite sure?' she said slowly. 'I thought it was because he wanted me to work late. But then we left at once, so...'

'Maybe he wants you to go away with him,' said Andrew, pursuing his own line of thought.

Sally dropped the spoon, spraying coffee granules all over the counter-top.

'That's ridiculous,' she said breathlessly. 'Why on earth should he?'

Andrew looked surprised. 'To type some secret report. Or help out with some super-confidential business deal. They meet in all sorts of places, you know. Hotels in the south of France so people will think they're on holiday—that sort of thing. He might want you to go— and Gramps and I could come along as camouflage.'

Sally ruffled his hair. 'You're an opportunist,' she told him.

But her smile was twisted. Andrew had the instincts of a traveller, like their father. And he was a born linguist too. She had managed to afford for him to go with the school to France the year before, but this year it was impossible. They had to have the house rewired. There was simply not the money to do both.

Andrew, however, was unaware of tragedy. He grinned back at her.

They carried the coffee back into the sitting-room. Paul sprang to his feet to take the tray from her, watched disapprovingly by her grandfather. In the hall the telephone rang.

Andrew went to answer it, returning to say portentously that it was Old Joe from the allotments. Grandfather was galvanised. Virtually brushing Andrew aside, he shot into the hall, forgetting his walking-stick.

Since it would be impossible for him to prop himself up while he talked to his crony on the wall-mounted telephone, Andrew picked up the walking-stick and took it out to him.

Sally looked after him, frowning. He seemed spry enough indoors. But recently he had been showing more and more reluctance to go out. He assured her there was nothing wrong—but she couldn't help wondering.

Paul accepted coffee and drank it absently. He never, Sally noticed with unease, took his eyes off her.

At last he said, 'Have you ever wanted to marry, Sally?'

She gulped and a mouthful of hot coffee hit her windpipe. It made a reply impossible for the next few seconds, which was just as well. She could not have been more startled if he'd picked her up and held her out of the window. Paul watched her interestedly.

At last she could breathe again. She put the mug down.

'Why on earth do you ask me that?'

He shrugged. 'Have you?'

Sally said levelly, 'I don't think that's any of your business.'

It was a question that most people were too tactful to ask. Not that considerations of tact would deter Paul

Theokaris if he wanted to know something, Sally thought wryly. Normally she could deal with his startling frankness. But this was a sensitive subject.

On the one hand there was her family: financially and emotionally dependent on her. As Aunt Mary, the friend who had long ago appointed herself the conscience of the family, pointed out, what man would want to marry Sally and take on a ready-made burden like that?

There was also, though Sally had carefully concealed it from everyone, the dark memories she had of her fierce, charismatic father and a mother so desperately in love with him that she would endure anything at his hands. No one was ever, Sally had promised herself from her adolescence onwards, going to get her in his power like that.

But the really sensitive issue—the tender spot that made her wince to think about it—was her secret and wholly impracticable dreams about himself. She was slightly ashamed of them and certainly did not want to see them exposed to the light of the day. And, if she did, Paul Theokaris was the last person on earth she would have chosen to confide in.

Paul said slowly, 'You know that my family want me to marry. It's not just Costas.'

Now completely thrown, Sally said blankly, 'Good grief.' Then, as he looked at her steadily, she couldn't resist. 'Why?'

He gave a low laugh. 'Stability. Responsible adulthood. Carrying on the dynasty. That's what they *say*. What they mean is a family man will be more indissolubly tied to the firm.'

It sounded a pretty long shot to Sally.

In spite of her determination not to invite personal confidences, she said, 'Do you want to?'

His eyes slid away from hers. He looked very dark and untrustworthy.

'Not quite just at the moment, no.'

Sally strove with her baser self and lost. Curiosity was too strong.

'Who...?'

'Who do they want me to marry?'

She nodded.

'Anyone. Preferably young and healthy, of course.' He sounded cynical.

To her surprise, Sally thought he also sounded almost hurt. She was not often moved to comfort Paul Theokaris, whom she regarded dispassionately as being too handsome, too intelligent and altogether too charming, but she was moved now.

But all she said was, 'They must have someone in mind.'

He lifted his shoulders. 'A nice young girl. I told you.'

The glinting smile was world-weary. Sally had the sudden inexplicable impression of an immense tiredness beneath the charm. She didn't know what to say.

She stood up and began to collect the debris that generally attended Grandfather's television viewing. Paul watched her with an odd little smile.

'You're right,' he said as if she had spoken. 'A nice young girl isn't really me. A sensible woman, now...' He let the phrase trail off, mischievously.

For a moment Sally did not catch the implication. Even when she did, she stared, not really believing that he could say what he seemed to be saying.

He stood up. The dark eyes were opaque, but Sally had a nasty feeling there was a message there if she was skilled enough to read it. He took the papers and orange peel from her hands.

'A business arrangement,' he said rapidly. 'You're carrying an awful lot by yourself.' He did not look down at the unsavoury load in his hands. He did not have to.

'I can help. If you were to marry me you'd have to let me help with all this.'

Sally sat down heavily. She felt as if someone had taken a mallet to her stomach and knocked all the wind out of her.

'I'm afraid I'm not that sensible,' she said at last.

And at that moment Andrew came back into the room. Paul looked impatient, with a quick, fierce drawing together of his brows.

Sally knew the look and her heart sank. She had seen it all too often and knew it presaged an explosion. She did not feel up to deflecting that anger from Andrew. Nor did she think she could bear to withstand Paul Theokaris if he was determined to persuade her to marry him at a full family council. He was quite capable of it, Sally knew well.

'We can talk about it later if you like,' she said hastily.

It was, she thought afterwards, her first mistake.

CHAPTER TWO

SALLY didn't, of course, get to the PTA meeting until the place was three-quarters empty and a hopeful gym master was stacking chairs. The headmistress greeted her severely.

'It's a shame you couldn't get here earlier, Miss Harrison. I know Mr Padgett was hoping for a word.'

Sally bent her head ruefully. 'I'm sorry,' she murmured. 'I got held up at work.'

The headmistress unbent. There were all too many single parents in Sally's position, and she was not an unreasonable woman.

'Well, perhaps you could have a word with him on the telephone, Miss Harrison. Can you ring from work? He has a double free period before lunch tomorrow. You might catch him then.'

Sally's heart sank.

'Is it about the school trip to France?' she asked with foreboding.

But Miss Firmin was vague. She knew it was nothing for Miss Harrison to worry about. Andrew was coming along splendidly: a difficult time for a boy, of course, but he seemed very sensible, with a real talent for languages.

'Thank you,' said Sally, trying to be pleased.

The other teachers were brisk and to the point. Andrew worked well when he was interested and was hell on earth when he wasn't. It was clear to Sally that he was giving the biology mistress a hard time. She promised to have a word with him and left.

It was crazy, she thought wryly, that she could deal
with Andrew's bad behaviour without too much worry
while the headmistress's compliments on his work sent
her into a flat spin. She sighed. Andrew needed his
chance. His father had had it. But how on earth was she
going to find the money?

She was still preoccupied by the problem when she
arrived at work. It filled her mind to such an extent that
she had almost forgotten her wariness following Paul
Theokaris's crazy suggestion of the previous evening.
Almost.

It came rushing back to her the moment she set eyes
on him. It stopped her dead in the doorway of his office.
She would have to be very careful, she thought. She knew
what he was like when he wanted something. If he decided to use some of his devastating negotiating tech-
niques on her she would have to call on all her self-
possession to resist him.

To her consternation, the blood rushed to her cheeks
as it had not last night. She avoided his eyes. But she
knew there was unholy amusement in them.

There was nothing else in his demeanour to suggest
that he noticed her confusion—or even that he remembered the conversation that had caused it. This was not,
she thought bitterly, because he was chivalrous, but because he had other things on his mind.

He was in his shirt-sleeves, talking to Tokyo. He
looked as if he'd been up all night.

Quietly she gave him coffee. He sent her an absent
smile. So much for over-persuasion, thought Sally wryly.
She was relieved, of course. But was there the faintest
hint of disappointment underneath? For a few crazy
minutes last night, looking round at the last lingering
couples at the PTA meeting, she had allowed herself to
dream what it would be like to have someone to lean
on.

Paul Theokaris to lean on, she reminded herself. Too handsome, too intelligent, too charming. As a steady reliable father substitute, he didn't even make it into the qualifying rounds. Who should know that better than his confidential secretary?

Sally went back to her desk. She propped her chin on her hands, thinking about the glamorous women who regularly drifted past her desk on their way to Paul. He didn't seem to have to try very hard, she thought ruefully. He forgot birthdays and cancelled dates with monotonous regularity. And he went from one girl to another with a speed which would have been indecent if he hadn't been so open about it.

None of the girlfriends could ever say he misled them, either. Nobody had exclusive rights. He made no secret of the fact. Most of them seemed to accept it without complaint. Presumably they thought his lavish gifts were adequate compensation, Sally thought cynically. Nobody could say he was generous about the time he spent with them.

Being in love with a man like that would be hell, Sally reflected. She shivered. But another thought was stirring at the bottom of her mind as well: What would it be like to be married to him?

Her reverie was interrupted by a small whirlwind. Paul stormed out of his office and stood over her, hands braced at each corner of the desk. His heavy brows were drawn together in a straight line. He looked fighting mad. Sally braced herself.

But she was not the focus of his anger.

'Do you know what that old fool's done now?' he demanded. 'He's gone and ordered another ship—did it while he was in Japan. When we can't fill the ones we've got.'

Sally knew the current financial state of the company. This was appalling.

'Oh, lord,' she said with feeling.

Paul straightened, pushing an impatient hand through his hair.

'Is that all you can say? I've been on the phone most of the night. Nobody seems to know what happened.'

'Perhaps it isn't as bad...' said Sally without much hope.

Costas was high-handed and energetic, with a sense of judgement that had brought the company to the brink on more than one occasion. It was for that reason that they had sent out an SOS for Paul when his father died. Paul had quickly curbed Costas's powers with the result that the older man was bored out of his skull much of the time. If he was let loose somewhere like Tokyo she could just imagine the sort of deal he would start setting up.

Paul said, 'I told them not to let him out of their sight. The fools. The blasted fools. They don't know what happened, but Mr Theokaris assured them he had full signing powers...'

He banged his fist down on her desk so hard that he hurt himself. 'Ouch.' He turned the hand over, examining it. Sally had to repress an urge to offer comfort.

'Hell. There's not much I can do. At least not until I find out how bad it is.' He sounded grim. 'I've just got hold of our lawyers in Tokyo to see what exactly Costas has signed.'

'How could he?' said Sally involuntarily. 'He knows how things stand. And if you'd wanted a new ship you'd have taken it to the management committee.'

Paul sighed. His temper seemed to have spent itself. 'Costas doesn't believe in committees. He thinks they get in the way of doing what he wants. Which,' he added with a touch of his normal humour, 'they usually do, thank heaven. On this occasion, I gather, some sharp operator took him on a tour of the sights of Osaka, ending up in a famous bar with a saki in one hand and a contract in the other. Costas was enjoying himself. So,' Paul shrugged, 'he signed.'

'How did you find out?'

He flashed her his sudden grin. It was always unexpected and it made him look like a particularly wicked demon king enjoying himself. As always, Sally felt her lips twitch in response.

'Contacts.' He gave a small private laugh. 'Someone in the same line of business happened to ask me last night whether it was true we were ordering a new cruise ship from Japan. I came straight back here and called some people out there.'

'Last night?'

'Well, the small hours. Daylight in Japan. Don't forget, there isn't a lot of overlap.' He looked at his watch. 'They'll all be off to their karaoke bars about now.'

Sally said, 'So we'll have to wait till tomorrow to find out what Costas has done?'

Paul looked affronted. 'Of course not. I told the lawyer to keep at it until he found out. He'll be ringing back today.'

Sally said hesitantly, 'You could ask Costas.'

'I have.'

'And what did he say?'

'Moaned about being got out of bed at three in the morning and complained about my morals,' Paul retorted promptly.

Sally gaped at him.

'For being awake at three,' he explained.

'Ah.'

Sally looked down at her notebook. Presumably Paul had not been alone and Costas had detected it.

Even since Paul had joined the company his uncle had appointed himself his mentor. There were more fights about Paul's girlfriends and after-hours activities than there were about the business. And there were plenty about the business. It made for an unrestful atmosphere.

Paul looked down at her bent head. 'You're very discreet,' he said, amused.

'Well, it's not really my business,' she murmured, making meaningless squiggles on her shorthand pad.

Paul's face darkened. 'Any more than it's Costas's. Lord knows what right he thinks he's got to lecture me. Anyone would think he's been a pillar of the community, the way he goes on. Instead of a drunken, devious, irresponsible old idiot.'

Sally nodded without speaking. There was obviously going to be additional bite to today's exchange between uncle and nephew.

Paul gave a soft laugh. 'There's only one pillar of the community round here, isn't there, Sally, my love?' She looked up quickly. He pinched her cheek. 'And you don't approve of either of us.'

She removed his hand from her cheek and gave it back to him. Standing up, she said, 'I'm not paid to approve.'

'Not part of your secretarial duties?' Paul sounded almost annoyed. 'But you must have *some* feelings. Even a perfect secretary like you.'

For a hectic moment Sally debated telling him what she really thought of him and his uncle and their feuding. Then she caught hold of herself.

'There's not a lot of room for anybody else's feelings round here,' she pointed out drily. 'You and your uncle take up most of the available space. And I'm——'

'Not paid to feel. I know. I know.' Paul looked at her speculatively. 'But I swear there's *something* that——'

He stopped, an arrested expression on his face. Sally looked at him enquiringly.

'Something?'

A smile she didn't like was flickering about the corners of his mouth. Paul Theokaris looked like a cat who had just remembered that he had discovered exclusive access to the family's cream supply.

'Oh, nothing,' he said unconvincingly. 'What's in the diary today?'

Sally flicked the screen on to the diary page and told him.

'And the others?'

She gave him Costas's timetable, the finance director's and half a dozen others' at his request.

'And this evening?'

She primmed her mouth. It was her private opinion that Paul could manage to keep track of the ladies he was dating for himself. But he always insisted on every appointment going into the central diary. He said it was so that he could be contacted if there was an emergency, but it was Sally's private theory that it was because he wanted someone else to remind him when to wear his dinner-jacket, buy chocolates for his hostess and send flowers to his escorts.

She consulted the screen.

'Dinner with Mrs Glencairn before Katherine's dance,' she read out. 'You're escorting Amanda Carrier. You've said you'll pick her up at eight.'

The Glencairns were shareholders and old friends. Miss Carrier was a petite blonde with a breathless manner and an eye for diamonds. She had figured in Paul's diary for three or four months now. This would be the first time that he had taken her to a friend's house, though. Sally wondered briefly if he was serious about Amanda Carrier and winced.

Resolutely reminding herself that his social life was none of her business, she looked up at him.

'Chocolates for Mrs Glencairn?'

Paul nodded. 'Yes, please. I've got Katherine's birthday present. Now what about the fair Amanda?'

His mouth curved as he said the name. Sally looked at him with dudgeon. He sounded amused and affectionate but not the slightest bit serious. She found herself hoping quite viciously that one day he would fall for a lady who set him back in his tracks. Let him be amused and superior then!

She said brusquely, 'That's for you to decide.'

He leaned against the wall, arms crossed over his chest, watching her with interest.

'Well, you're a woman, aren't you?' he said in an injured tone. 'You can give me a bit of guidance. What would *you* like if I took you out to dinner?'

He was teasing her, Sally realised. He was a master at it and he thought she was too prim. Well, he was asking for it.

She met his eyes limpidly and said, 'Food.'

The dark eyes danced.

'Naturally. But what about the graceful token of my esteem to go with it?'

Sally shook her head. 'I can't imagine it,' she said drily.

Paul's face softened. 'Poor Sally. Am I such a brute?'

'There aren't a lot of graceful gestures,' she agreed.

'I stand rebuked. But I still need your assistance. If I were somebody else who did make graceful gestures to you—what would you like?'

Sally stared at him suspiciously. But he seemed perfectly serious. So she shrugged and thought about it.

'Oh, flowers, I suppose.'

Paul's face stayed calm and interested. 'Orchids?'

Sally shook her head. 'They're beautiful, of course, but they always look as if they're going to bite. If it were me I'd rather have something wonderful that smells. Lilac or freesias.' She thought of the untidy, homely house and grinned suddenly. 'Something I could put on my bedside table and wake up to the scent.'

Paul made a small sound of surprise. She looked up from her reverie, startled. He was wearing a curious expression.

'Sally Harrison, you're a closet romantic.'

For no reason at all that she could think of, she blushed. Paul continued to stare at her as if fascinated.

'Shall I order orchids for Miss Carrier?' she said hurriedly.

'What? Oh. No. No, I think Amanda will be looking for something more—tangible.'

Her eyebrows flew up. Paul laughed softly.

'No, not diamond bracelets, you little cynic. I'm well aware of the lady's tastes. But she's not that close a friend—not yet, anyway. I was thinking of something from Insurrection.'

Sally nodded and made a note. The shop was a small one run by a couple of young designers who had attracted Paul's attention at some craft fair. He had decided to back their work and they now sold their quirky jewellery out of a smart little West End boutique. A little was made of precious stones but mostly they worked in coral and jet and malachite. When Paul wanted to make a present to one of his girlfriends or innumerable female relatives they would send round a selection for him to choose from.

'I'll ring them.'

He looked oddly mischievous. 'Tell them lapis lazuli to go with her eyes.'

Sally thought of Amanda Carrier's hard blue gaze.

'If you want to match her eyes you'd do better with diamonds,' she said involuntarily.

Paul laughed out loud. He was as quick as a fox at picking up the ill-considered remark.

'Cat,' he said approvingly.

He went back into his office, whistling. It left Sally with the uneasy feeling—one she had had all too often since she'd started working for Paul Theokaris—that she had been outgunned by an expert. She rang the jewellers, organised the meeting he wanted and attacked the post.

It was midday when she stopped to ring Andrew's form master. She half hoped he wouldn't be there but he came to the phone at once.

'Thank you for calling,' he said formally. 'I wanted to talk to you about the school trip. . .'

Sally sighed. She earned a good salary but it was supporting three people and an old house that was falling down about their ears. She had done the sums over and over again and there was no way she could squeeze out enough for Andrew to go to France again without forgoing the rewiring that she knew was essential. There were bare wires showing behind some of the kitchen appliances, and when Andrew turned on the old fire in his room it gave off sparks.

She explained.

He tutted. 'But couldn't you borrow the money, Miss Harrison? I don't think you realise what a critical time this is for him. He's very good but if the rest of the class go and he doesn't he'll fall behind and then he could lose his motivation.'

That had not occurred to Sally.

'Do you think it's likely?' she asked anxiously.

The form master was a scrupulous man. 'Possible. He's not a great self-disciplinarian.'

'I know. But borrowing. . .' Sally bit her lip. 'I don't know when I could pay it back. As it is, I've got the mortgage and loans on the washing-machine and the boiler.'

'What about godfathers, grandparents, friends?'

Sally sighed. Her parents' friends had all been university teachers like themselves and had no spare cash. Gramps, with his old-age pension, was the only relative she and Andrew had living. And her own friends—well, she couldn't ask them. They didn't have any cash to spare and she didn't want their pity.

'Or maybe you could come to some arrangement with your employer?' the form master suggested, sensing her unresponsiveness. 'A lot of firms make educational loans.'

Sally made a face. The Theokaris empire was a relatively good employer, fair and honourable, but Paul was constantly reminding his personnel director that it was not a charitable institution. And she knew, none better, that it was going through hard times at the moment. Likely now, of course, to be harder since Costas's intervention.

But she had to say something to Andrew's teacher.

'My employer doesn't have a welfare scheme like that. But I'll ask,' she said, not meaning it. 'It's good of you to take so much trouble,' she added. She did mean that.

'Not at all. He's the brightest in the class by a long way,' the man said warmly. 'Leonard Harrison was your father, wasn't he? Andrew must take after him.'

Sally repressed a shiver. Please heaven, no.

'Yes,' she said quietly.

'That man was brilliant. I went to a series of lectures he gave in Arles. He was an inspiration.'

Sally remembered her father, the fierce eyes that had looked through his children and the quick, expressive hands that could strike out... She swallowed hard.

'Thank you.'

'We must do whatever we can for his son.'

'Of course,' she said without expression. 'I'll—be in touch.'

She put the phone down. Sending Andrew to France was beginning to seem imperative. But there was no way she could make the money stretch. She had done the sums over and over again in her head. She woke up thinking about them. But she was only just making ends meet as it was.

A small sound made her look up. Paul was lounging in the doorway of his room, one shoulder propped against the frame. From his expression Sally guessed he had been there some time. She bit her lip, annoyed. It made her feel vulnerable.

'Welfare scheme?' he echoed gently.

She glared at him. 'My brother's school thinks I ought to touch the company for the money to send him to France,' she snapped.

The strongly marked brows rose. He gave a soft laugh, strolling forward.

'And you told them not a chance,' he said approvingly.

If she had hoped softer feelings might prompt him to offer the money she would have been cruelly disappointed, Sally mused. It was just as well she knew him as well as she did. She gave him a sweet smile and brought up the subject she had been rigorously repressing all morning

'I ought to marry you and make you send Andrew round the world,' she told him.

His eyes gleamed. 'You should indeed.'

The idea was so unlikely that she laughed aloud. No matter what he'd said last night—and goodness knew what had prompted him to say it—a sophisticated sybarite with a taste for the Amanda Carriers of this world was not going to marry into a terraced house in an outer suburb, she realised.

He chuckled and picked up the blue file of the day's Press cuttings, newly arrived on her desk. There were a couple of pieces on the share price, a supplement on the international tanker fleet, a couple of gossip-column inches on his stepmother's entry into a Swiss sanatorium and a photograph of himself wrapped round a champagne bottle and a blonde from one of the glossy weeklies. Jo in Press Cuttings would have enjoyed putting that in.

Paul stopped when he came to it. Sally maintained a calm front. He gave her a guileless look, put his head on one side, considering the photograph's merits, and then screwed it up and lobbed it accurately at the wastepaper basket.

'Sally...'

The internal phone buzzed. It was Jane Drummond, Costas's secretary.

'Problem,' she said. 'I've had Stephanie on the phone and she's coming in. Now.'

'Oh,' said Sally, her heart sinking.

She looked up. Paul was already on his way out of the door. No help there.

Stephanie Cornelius had been three years old when her mother had married George Theokaris. She had been treated as the adored baby daughter ever since. She was now twenty-two, bored and beautiful and, in Sally's private opinion, spoiled rotten. When she was in London, which fortunately was not often, she expected Paul and Costas to make her their first priority. Paul, to be fair, generally took her to a party or two, but the rest he delegated to Costas.

'Why?'

'Apparently her mother's ill and she's feeling lonely,' Jane said without expression.

'She never *sees* her mother,' Sally began, then stopped. 'You mean she's over-spent her allowance?'

Jane's shrug was almost audible. 'I'd put money on it.'

Sally sighed. 'OK. Head her in this direction.'

'Bless you. I owe you,' Jane said, ringing off.

Sally stayed at her post throughout the lunch-hour. Stephanie did not turn up.

Normally Sally would have taken her lunch into the garden square in front of the building. She hated to eat at her desk. But today she spent the enforced period of sentry duty working and reworking her budget. She always got the same answer.

Eventually there came a mighty banging of doors and sounds of raised voices. Sally picked the memorandum sheet on which she had recorded incoming calls out of her typewriter.

Paul stormed into the office and through into his own room without speaking. Sally sat still and counted to twenty. He came out again.

'Has Tokyo called?'

She shook her head.

'Get me Wilberforce.'

He retreated into his lair again. Before he'd closed his door Sally was dialling the lawyers. In less than a minute he was connected and she sat back.

The door from the corridor opened and a girl dressed from head to foot in black leather appeared. She looked thin and pinched and her pallor was frightening. Sally, who knew that the waif look was achieved at substantial cost of time and money, surveyed her without enthusiasm.

'Hello, Stephanie.'

Miss Cornelius gave her a wavering smile. It would have been pathetic if it had done anything to soften the steely glitter of her huge brown eyes.

'Hello, Sally. Is Paul in?'

'No,' said Sally, crossing her fingers under the desk.

From his office there came the unmistakable sound of a telephone being slammed down. Stephanie made for his door.

'I wouldn't,' Sally advised neutrally.

Stephanie was not used to being told what to do—and indeed never complied when she was—but Sally's indifferently voiced advice had tended to be sound in the past. She looked round enquiringly.

'Bad day, bad deal,' Sally explained.

Stephanie hesitated, looking at the door. The doting older generation generally gave her whatever she wanted, but Paul, though undeniably sexy, had shown an unwelcome tendency to resist on occasions. She went back to Sally's desk.

'I need to see him,' she said simply.

'Cash-flow problems?' asked Sally. 'I can sort that out for you temporarily. You can talk to Paul later.'

Stephanie shook her head. 'No. It's not money. Or not *yet*,' she added obscurely.

'Well, he's pretty tied up with the company at the moment...'

'This is *my* company too,' Stephanie said unexpectedly.

Sally stared.

Stephanie gave a little giggle. 'Don't look like that. I'm not going to come and work here. But the lawyers have been talking to me about my inheritance. And I need to talk it over with Paul.'

Sally nodded slowly. She did not know the provisions of George Theokaris's will, but it was reasonable enough that the beloved stepdaughter would inherit some part of his empire.

'I'll tell Paul. Where are you staying?'

Stephanie made a face. 'I'm at the Berkeley at the moment. That horrid man wouldn't let me into the flat.'

Anne Theokaris had rented out her Mayfair apartment for a year at an exorbitant rent. It had clearly not occurred to Stephanie that this made it unavailable to her when she descended on London at her usual half-day's notice. Sally sighed.

'I expect I'll go and stay with Paul in the end,' she added blithely.

Sally kept her inevitable thoughts to herself. She had never had the impression that Paul was more than impatiently fond of his stepmother's child and she was reasonably sure that he would not want any member of his family moving in with him. It would, she thought wryly, cramp his style.

'I'll tell him,' she promised.

Stephanie drifted out.

Sally checked that Paul was still on the telephone, put an automatic call on to connect them when he finished, and rang Jane.

'You wouldn't have any coffee on?'

Jane chuckled. 'The young master forgotten that slaves need sustenance? I'll bring it up.'

She was as good as her word. In minutes she was there with two mugs of freshly brewed coffee. Jane perched on the edge of Sally's desk.

'How's the crush?'

It was an old joke. When Paul Theokaris had first brought Sally to the firm the other secretaries had been as wary of her as they were of the new boss. Eventually they had made overtures. And the first thing Jane had asked when they'd lunched together was, 'What's he like? How do you get on with him?'

'He's tall, dark and handsome and I've got a crush on him,' Sally had said composedly. She found it was always best to tell the truth. You had a reasonable chance people would not believe you.

Jane had certainly never believed her. And neither had Paul when, inevitably, it had got back to him. He had roared with laughter and told her she was bad for his image.

She said now drily, 'Wavering.'

'I'll bet.' Jane took a sip of coffee. 'How much did Stephanie cost the petty cash?'

Sally shook her head. 'Not money. She wanted to talk to Paul, but he was on the phone, so I sent her away.'

Jane sighed. 'You've got the magic touch. That must be why you work for the boss and I don't.'

Sally grinned at her. 'There's nothing difficult about dealing with Stephanie as long as you don't go for a trial of strength. And the reason I work for the boss, as you perfectly well know, is that I'm much too dull and unglamorous to get ideas about him. And you're not.'

Jane chuckled, tossing her tawny streaked head.

'You choose to be unglamorous,' she said calmly. 'If you wanted to you could knock their socks off. You've got wonderful skin and the most gorgeous green eyes I've ever seen.' She grinned suddenly. 'It would be wonderful to see the young master's face if you did a transformation scene one day.'

Sally kept her face calm. It was a fantasy which had occurred to her, too, over the last four years, and she always suppressed it firmly. Quite apart from the fact that she didn't want his laughing at her, she didn't want to lose a good job. And if he didn't laugh at her—well, she didn't think she could handle that. On his past record his intentions would be strictly dishonourable.

Drily—and truthfully—she said, 'He could probably take it. It's me that couldn't.'

'OK, Cinderella. I give up. This time.' Jane unhitched herself from the desk and moved off. 'But one day you'll let me do something about your clothes—and you won't know yourself.'

Sally laughed. 'That could be uncomfortable,' she said to the closing door.

For a moment she sat and looked at it, her imagination flying. Paul always called her Sensible Sally, like some sort of rag doll, and she hated it. It would be wonderful—just once—to be glamorous, witty Sally; to shake him out of his cool control; to take the teasing laughter out of him and make him treat her as a woman. Just once.

'Except I couldn't handle it,' said Sally out loud. 'Damn, damn, damn.'

CHAPTER THREE

THE Tokyo call came through at three. The agent sounded exhausted. It would be early morning, Sally calculated compassionately. He must have been up all night. Paul certainly was imperious in his demands. Paul, however, sounded less than appreciative when he ordered her curtly to put it through.

He stayed invisible in his room for the rest of the day. He made a number of calls to bankers, not just in London. His temper got steadily worse. Sally gave silent thanks that she did not actually have to sit in the room with him.

The jewellers' selection arrived and she signed for it. It was not, she assured them, the time to go and display their wares in person to Mr Theokaris. She put the neat briefcase on one side and waited for the atmosphere to improve.

At six she debated with herself. Paul did not normally take out his ill temper on her, no matter how furious he was. It was still an act of courage to square her shoulders and go quietly into his office.

He had the high-backed swivel chair swung away from her, so that he could look out over the tree-tops of the garden square. Sally hesitated, unable to see his expression. She had thought he was on the telephone, but the handset dangled, as if he had flung it away from him. She went calmly to the desk and restored it to its cradle.

It was unlike him to fling office machinery about. His uncle Costas regularly broke filing cabinets and photo-

40

copiers. But when Paul got angry he went quiet and precise and very, very controlled. Something was very wrong indeed.

She looked at the still figure, lost in its reverie, with concern.

'Is there anything I can do?' she asked quietly.

For a moment the figure seemed to freeze. She realised that he had not known she was there. That in itself was unprecedented. He had the hearing of a bat and the self-protective instincts of a tiger. Then, very slowly, he swivelled the chair round to face her.

'What's wrong?' Sally said instinctively, catching sight of his face.

Paul shook his head. He seemed almost dazed.

'Costas not only signed the contract. He had witnesses,' Paul told her in a voice of stone.

'He must have been out of his mind,' Sally gasped.

'No.' His tone was very precise. 'Just drunk. And out with his good friends the Mariscoffs.'

'But——'

Paul sent her a grim look. 'Quite.'

The Mariscoffs owned Theokaris Lines's major rival. Sally shook her head. 'But surely—I mean, the supplier...'

'The supplier is very sorry,' Paul said, still in that clipped, emotionless voice. 'He will do what he can to compromise. But times are hard, even in Japan, and his firm needs the order.'

Sally blinked. 'What are you going to do?'

Paul stared at her as if he couldn't see her.

'There isn't anything I *can* do. I could modify the contract for the ship—but I still have to order some sort of vessel. I can't afford to back out of it altogether. You pay the compensation and have nothing to show for it. And I can't pay for the ship unless the bankers agree. You'd have thought,' he added with the first spark of feeling he had shown, 'that Costas would at least have remembered that you talk to the people who lend you the money *before* you buy the damned thing.'

Sally realised suddenly why he had been on the telephone all afternoon.

'The bankers won't lend?'

Paul gave a sigh that was almost a groan. He stretched, grimacing.

'They want to talk about it. That means they'll only lend at a price.' He passed his weary hand over his eyes. 'Maybe I can't afford that either.'

'When are you seeing them?'

He stood up. 'Seven-fifteen tomorrow at the Savoy. Let Alan know, will you?'

Sally nodded. It was not the first time the finance director had been called in from his rural home for a breakfast meeting. And after today's management meeting he must be expecting something of the kind.

'And—er—your uncle?'

'If I see Costas again I might just murder him,' Paul said coldly. 'If you want to retain your reputation as a peacemaker, keep him out of my sight.'

'Right,' said Sally, meaning it. 'Anything else?'

He sent her a wry look. 'Whatever's in the diary tomorrow, you'd better cancel it. I suppose you've already dealt with today's.'

Sally remembered his stepsister.

'All but one. Stephanie's at the Berkeley and she wants to see you.'

Paul said something very rude. Sally looked down at her notepad and said nothing.

'Oh, and what about the Glencairn dance? Should I ring Miss Carrier and apologise?'

'Good lord, no.' He looked horrified.

Sally was moved to protest. 'But you're exhausted. You've been up all night and you look dead.'

Paul shrugged. 'So I have a second sleepless night.'

Sally, about to tell him roundly he was an idiot, suddenly thought of the blonde and beautiful Amanda and why tonight might also be sleepless. She subsided, rather flushed.

'By the time I get to the Oxford marmalade the adrenalin should be at maximum,' Paul said cynically. 'It'll do wonders for my powers of persuasion.'

Sally primmed her mouth and prepared to depart.

'Insurrection's sent round some things for you to look at. For Miss Carrier's present,' she reminded him.

She thought he would be impatient but instead he looked interested.

'Wheel them in, then. I don't have a lot of time.' He looked at his watch. 'I'll have hell's own job to get back home and change as it is.'

'There's a dinner-jacket in the flat,' Sally volunteered. 'I don't know about a shirt. I could check, if you like.'

He looked startled, then warmly amused.

'What a wonderful secretary you are, Sensible Sally. Always resourceful. Go and check it out, would you, darling, while I look at the tinsel?'

She winced at the casual endearment. She was sure he knew it annoyed her and did it deliberately.

'Certainly,' she said stiffly. And went.

The flat was a small two-bedroom affair next to the engine house on the roof of the building. It was used by executives staying unexpectedly overnight in London. Occasionally there was a private meeting in its designer drawing-room, mainly when the Theokaris family were falling out about their dividends, in Sally's experience.

Paul and his uncle used it to change quite often before they went to City dinners. There were several suits hanging in the wardrobe of the palatial master suite. She located his dinner-jacket without trouble and even found a clean ruffled shirt, though it plainly needed a press.

She knew where the iron was and plugged it in. The flat was well equipped with linen and she got a couple of fluffy towels and a fresh bar of soap out of the cupboard for Paul. Then she buzzed him on the internal telephone.

'You're in luck. Everything's here. I'm just ironing your shirt.'

On reflection she should not have said that, she realised. It made him laugh. He said in the mock sexy, husky murmur that made her grit her teeth, 'Wonderful. Now all you need to do is start running my bath and I'll be with you at once.'

Sally closed her eyes, counted to ten, opened her eyes and said crisply, 'Executive baths are not part of my job description, Mr Theokaris. You're on your own with the rubber ducks.'

He was still laughing when she put the phone down and marched into the small kitchen.

The iron took an age to warm up. Sally found a can of spray starch and decided to do a proper job on his dress shirt. She did not have much of a chance with Andrew, who liked his clothes old, limp and preferably grimy.

She heard him come into the flat, whistling. He went straight to the master bedroom and she heard the water swoosh through the pipes as he drew his own bath. An experience for him, she thought acidly, pushing the iron over the crisp frills with quite unnecessary vigour. She shook the shirt out and hung it on a surprisingly feminine hanger covered with pink velvet and a pomander. The flowery scent would clash with his aftershave, she thought with satisfaction.

Sally hunted through the kitchen cupboards and found some elderly herbal tea. No milk, of course, but it would be wet and warm and she needed it. She put through a quick call to Gramps while she waited for it to brew. He was unsurprised.

'Young Theokaris bringing you home?' he asked hopefully.

'No. He's out on the town with a real girlfriend,' Sally said repressively.

Gramps snorted. She thought he said, 'More fool you,' but she couldn't be sure. Anyway, she didn't want to press it.

There were no further sounds from the bedroom, so she took the shirt through. There were no sounds from the bathroom either. He'd probably gone to sleep in the warm water, Sally thought, with a flicker of compassion. She picked up the jumble of cloth that was his Savile-Row-tailored business suit and began to smooth the creases out of the jacket.

And he walked out of the bathroom, rubbing his face with a towel. His hair was curly and his body glistened with the damp. His bare feet made rather neat Man Friday footprints on the grey carpet. She noticed it, frozen to the spot. The rest of him was bare too.

Sally dropped the suit she was holding and blushed to the tips of her ears.

For a moment Paul stood perfectly still, his face blank. Then one eyebrow flew up and he whisked the towel decorously round him, knotting it at the waist. That still left Sally confronting a bare, muscular chest and eyes that were frankly amused.

He did not have the body of a City businessman, Sally thought involuntarily. He looked like an athlete—and a powerful one. Why didn't I realise what all that squash would do to his shoulder muscles? It was the only thought that surfaced out of the embarrassed whirlpool of her mind. That, of course, only made her the more embarrassed.

'I thought you were in the bath,' she said angrily, conscious that she had no face left to save.

Paul's smile grew. 'Shower,' he said succinctly. 'It's more refreshing. And it conserves water in times of drought,' he added, looking smug.

Sally's blush began to subside.

'I should have thought. I'm sorry.'

'Don't be. My house is your house,' he told her teasingly.

Sally strove hard for composure, avoiding his eyes. She cleared a suddenly dry throat and looked down at the pile of sober pin-stripe she had dropped. 'I was trying to be helpful.' Her mouth quirked as she picked up the suit and began to shake it out again. 'Not very bright.'

The brown eyes were curiously intent.

'I wouldn't have said that,' Paul said softly.

He strolled over to and lifted the sleeve of his clean shirt on its hanger. It brought him a lot closer. It was a matter of pride for Sally not to flinch, though she could feel the warmth of his skin as he stood beside her.

'Very professional,' Paul said, fingering the cuff.

She had the impression that he was talking at random. He did it sometimes when he was struck by one of his inspirations: he would carry on conducting an ordinary conversation, but Sally, who knew him very well, knew that his mind was frantically busy, planning and examining something else. It usually meant a major piece of typing for her the following day. She could almost hear his mind working now.

Sally moved away from him, opening the cupboard door and busying herself with hanging up the maltreated suit. She concentrated on it with quite unnecessary intensity, trying to ignore the hint of the sandalwood soap he used that wafted across to her.

He was not looking at her. His eyes had turned inward on something new and—from his expression—intriguing.

Sally pulled herself together. She shut the cupboard door, turned back to him and said briskly, 'Well, I'll leave you to finish dressing. I——'

'Why?' Paul said softly.

'—made some tea and ... *What*?'

Paul turned his eyes on her, his smile mischievous. 'Why go? Stay and talk to me.'

Sally knew he was teasing—he thought it was amusing to tease her about her puritan outlook—but she still backed away until she came up against the cupboard door behind her.

She said firmly and as calmly as she could, 'I don't think that's a very good idea.'

His eyes were brilliant. He shook his head. 'I don't agree. You could look after my bowtie and my cuff-links.' The brown eyes were limpid with innocence. 'They're not easy to do on your own, you know. I'm not used to it.'

'That,' said Sally, hanging on to her temper, 'is your problem.'

Paul looked wounded. He took a step towards her. Sally became very conscious of the slatted cupboard door. She had retreated against it so hard that it was pressing into her shoulder-blades.

'But you're supposed to sort out my problems,' Paul pointed out. 'That's your job.'

She had a nasty feeling that he knew exactly how hard she was pressed against the cupboard door and was amused by it.

'Mr Theokaris——'

'You always call me that when you're angry with me,' he murmured.

He came another step closer. Sally had to tilt her head to look him in the face now. When she met his eyes, she wished she hadn't. Although they were dancing, there was some sort of deep purpose there. Innocent though

she was in general, Sally didn't have much doubt about
the nature of that purpose.

'I *told* you——' she began heatedly.

'I know.' It was soothing.

He put out a hand and curved the back of it down
her cheek, like someone testing the texture of a flower
petal. Sally caught her breath so sharply that she nearly
choked. The brown eyes locked with hers, smiling.

'I know,' he murmured in a teasing undervoice. 'No
rubber duck. No cuff-links. You wouldn't be a killjoy,
would you, Harrison?'

Sally resisted the temptation to shut her eyes and
scream.

'I'm not paid to do up your cuff-links.'

Paul put one muscular arm over her shoulder, bracing
himself against the cupboard door. He looked down at
her. He was not touching her but she could feel the vi-
brating warmth from his body from her head to her toes.
She turned her head away.

'You're not paid to iron my shirts either,' he pointed
out. 'But I didn't even have to ask.'

'That was out of the goodness of my heart,' Sally said
hastily, blushing.

He turned his hand over against the soft skin and
cupped her face. He brought her head gently round to
face him.

'Excellent. And what else might that generous heart
be persuaded to do, mm? If I *did* ask, I mean?' he murmured, his eyes on her mouth.

Sally gave up the struggle and shut her eyes briefly.

'You're not playing fair,' she said.

'No. But you knew I don't play fair.'

Sally opened her eyes and glared at him. The
handsome head was only a breath away, and she knew
she hadn't a chance of escape.

'You don't *do* this sort of thing with your secretaries,' she said, on a last desperate throw. 'You said so. You said it was a condition of working for you. No dalliance. You don't permit it.'

'No.' His expression was thoughtful. 'I don't, do I?'

And then his mouth closed softly but very firmly over hers and the battle was lost.

It would not be true to say that Sally had never been kissed before. But for reasons of her own she kept men at arm's length. She had certainly never been kissed by a nearly naked man with a reputation for being irresistible in three continents.

Her first thought after the initial shock was, This isn't as alarming as I thought. Her second, as his mouth feathered softly against her inside lip and she felt her whole body lean towards him on a sigh of yearning was, Oh, yes, it is.

As if he felt her reaction, Paul removed the arm that was bracing him against the cupboard behind her head and pulled her hard against him. His mouth stayed gentle but the hands that urged her forward were like iron.

Sally tried to say, Stop it, and felt his tongue flick wickedly against her own. She tried to push him away: but her hands encountered the wall of warm bone and muscle and curled into compliant paws against his skin. He made her feel warm and treasured and at the same time hopelessly vulnerable.

Years of practice, she assured herself, grimly. Hold on to that. He's had years of practice with women who knew what he was doing and had a better chance to defend themselves than you'd have in full armour. Remember his girlfriends and keep your head.

It wasn't easy. He was nibbling her earlobe, murmuring something in that husky, laughing tone that made her toes curl even when he was on the other end of a telephone and not talking to her. With a huge effort of will Sally wrenched her mind away from the seductive pleasure of his mouth against her skin and concentrated on listing the girlfriends she had seen.

There was the blonde Amanda, of course. And, before that, Sarah Gentian the dress designer. She'd been nice. Then there was the de la Tessière girl. He'd been skiing in her party a couple of years running. And the Australian girl. What *was* her name? A tall, broad-shouldered model-type with smouldering eyes...

Paul was placing the lightest of kisses along the soft curve of her throat. Involuntarily Sally's head fell back.

Dark, she thought frantically. She was very dark and tragic-looking. She had been pretty tragic when she looked at Paul, anyway. Even in his office on a grey winter afternoon, his secretary had been able to pick up the girl's hunger. Sally had winced away from it, angry with Paul that he could make someone suffer like that without conscience.

That was it. He had no conscience. If a woman allowed him to make love to her she did it at her own risk. It was a cold little thought. Sally strove to hang on to it.

'You're not concentrating,' Paul complained softly.

'Oh, yes, I am,' said Sally with real feeling.

He gave a soft laugh, not pretending to misunderstand. 'Counting sheep?'

She was wry. 'In a way.'

He looked down at her, the brown eyes alert.

'That doesn't sound very promising,' he said acutely.

'No,' she agreed, thankful.

Sally seemed to regain control of her limbs. She pushed at the naked chest with resolution. Watching her, he gave ground, though only a little. His eyes narrowed.

'It won't do any good, you know,' he said at last.

He spoke in his normal voice, quite unlike the husky whisper of the past few devastating minutes. It was such a contrast that Sally jumped.

'What won't?'

The slow smile was a challenge. Sally didn't like it.

'Counting whatever you were counting. What was it, by the way? Stationery? Work outstanding?'

Meeting all that confident amusement, Sally was suddenly furious. He had no right to look so pleased with himself, so *indifferent,* when he could reduce a girl to mindlessness just because he hadn't got anything better to do for a few minutes.

'Girlfriends,' she said coldly. 'Yours.'

Paul went very still. Then he gave a soft laugh.

'Clever,' he said approvingly.

'It worked,' Sally agreed.

She walked past him, not looking at him. He let her go. But she could feel his eyes on her and she knew what expression he would be wearing: thoughtful, assessing. She didn't like that either.

He said musingly, 'A masterly tactic. I'm impressed. You must have had a lot of practice. I wish I knew at what.'

She lifted the dress shirt, hanger and all, off its perch and held it out to him.

'You talk as if we're playing some sort of game,' she said from behind the barrier of the shirt.

'And aren't we?'

Sally shook her head decisively.

'Not me. I don't play games. And, if I did, I wouldn't play with *you.*'

He was undisturbed. 'Why not?' he asked as if he was really interested.

'Because I don't like your rules,' Sally goaded.

His brows flew up. 'Rules?'

He sounded so astonished that she rounded on him.

'Yes, rules. Conventions. Decent behaviour. Most people don't conduct their love-affairs like duels, you know, trying to beat their opponent into the ground. Most people like and respect and—and care for the people they...' She stopped, confused.

'Sleep with?' Paul supplied smoothly.

Sally glared at him. 'Yes.'

'You don't know what you're talking about.'

Her eyes flashed at his dismissive tone.

'And you do, I suppose?'

'Oh, yes,' said Paul tranquilly. 'I do.'

She realised she was still holding the shirt. She flung it down on the bed, careless of the creases, even after all her careful ironing.

'You're impossible.'

'I'm a realist,' said Paul.

Disconcerted, Sally found he was in front of her, barring her route to the door. She stood her ground but something began to flutter in the pit of her stomach as if she were afraid of him. Which was, of course, ridiculous.

'Take this evening,' Paul said gently. 'We've known each other for four years. Almost as intimately as it's possible to. You know my weaknesses and my tempers and my errors of judgement. You don't like or respect me. You certainly don't,' he echoed her words, '*care* for me. But——' And he shrugged.

Colour swept into Sally's face.

'Are you saying I'd have gone to bed with you?'

His eyes glinted.

'Are you saying you wouldn't?'

'You're out of your mind,' she gasped.

Suddenly his face set hard.

'And you're a fool,' Paul said curtly.

This time she did not see it coming. He had her neatly off her feet and on top of the fateful shirt before she even registered that he had moved. And then he was beside her.

This time his hands were not kind and his mouth was not gentle, but he made his point. Sally was horrified to find herself borne along on a surge of response at gale force.

She made one small protest. It sounded like a kitten's mew, she thought, disgusted. Then his mouth closed over hers and she had to concentrate on breathing to survive at all. The hands on her body were deft and experienced and in all too short a time she was writhing in desperation. Not to get away.

At last Paul lifted his head. His breathing, she saw detachedly, wasn't even ruffled. He rolled back on to one elbow and looked down at her. The brown eyes were flat. At least he didn't seem amused any more.

'You see?'

Sally shook her head in a daze. She was bewildered. Her body felt strange. She looked down at herself and realised that he had more than half removed her sober blouse. It was hanging off one shoulder. Her modest, pretty sprigged cotton bra had gone too and was somehow tangled under her. The neat dark hair had come undone and was all over her face. She pushed it back, struggling up on to her elbow.

'I suppose you think you've proved something . . .' she began heatedly.

He was perfectly relaxed now. The stony look had disappeared as if it had never been. Instead he looked, she thought angrily, distinctly pleased with himself.

'I'm certain of it.'

'Not to *my* satisfaction,' Sally said firmly.

A devilish light came into the brown eyes.

'No, I know. I'm sorry about that,' said Paul Theokaris outrageously. 'But you know how tight my schedule is this evening. Another time.'

Sally made a small, incoherent sound of fury. Embarrassment forgotten, she bounced off the bed, catching at her dishevelled garments and shovelling them back on anyhow.

'You delude yourself,' she said, wrenching buttons into place.

She looked down at him. He did not answer. He was lying there with his hands clasped behind his head and an expression of lazy satisfaction on his face that made her want to hit him.

'There's no need to look so smug,' Sally told him sharply. 'You've behaved disgracefully.'

He grinned.

'Yup.'

She restrained herself from stamping her foot.

'I'll let you have my resignation in the morning,' she told him.

That should wipe the smile off his face. She knew how completely he depended on her to organise his office. She had seen the chaos caused by all the susceptible secretaries who had preceded her.

Paul did not look concerned.

'Do that and I'll sue you for sexual harassment,' he said amiably.

Sally stared at him. He grinned back.

'Walking in on a man in his bath. Tripping around the kitchen of my living quarters ironing my linen. Uninvited. Think what a good lawyer could make of it,' he suggested, laughing.

Sally winced.

His voice dropped to that tempter's husky murmur. 'And without even giving me an answer.'

She was lost. 'Answer?'

'To my proposal of honourable matrimony,' said Paul. He chuckled, stretching. 'You see, you've forgotten. What my lawyer will make of *that*,' he said pleasurably.

'Any respectable man would have you written off as a cold-blooded tease in a minute.'

Sally stared at him blankly. She had finished doing up her buttons. She sat down rather suddenly on the first thing that came to hand. It happened to be the foot of the bed, but she was beyond noticing.

'You're not serious?' she said uncertainly. Her voice wavered.

There was a small pause. He still looked insultingly relaxed, lying there watching her. But his face was unreadable. And there was an oddly implacable set to the strong jaw that she knew. But surely he was not going to get into a trial of strength with her? She was no business rival, no threat to his independence. Yet there was something about the way he was looking at her...

She met his eyes, hers suddenly sober and a little beseeching, his opaque.

'You wouldn't—really?'

Paul seemed to debate his answer. For a moment his mouth twisted. Then he sat up and leaned towards her.

'You really do think I'm a bastard, don't you?' he mused. 'Now I wonder if that's office gossip or your own observation.'

Sally tried to stop her lip trembling.

'No.' It was very quiet. 'No, I wouldn't really.'

She drew a shaky breath.

'You had me worried for a minute.'

His eyes searched her face. 'So I see. You don't have much of an opinion of me, do you, Sally?'

She was regaining her equilibrium rapidly. 'You started it.'

'Yes,' he said, still quiet. 'Yes, I did, didn't I?'

He put out a hand and stroked a straying lock of hair back from her cheek. It was almost tender. Sally sat very still. Her heart began to slam against her ribs in slow, heavy blows that felt as if they would shake her apart. She felt as if she could hardly breathe. Her eyes fell.

'And are we going to finish it?' Paul said, almost to himself, Sally thought.

Not looking at him, she said in a high voice, 'If that means you want an answer to that ridiculous proposal of yours it's no.'

The silence was electric.

'Not,' she added defiantly, 'that I thought about it. It wasn't what *I'd* call a proposal. More a business proposition.'

'And what would you call a proposal?' Paul asked courteously after a pause that Sally felt through every atom of her body. He tipped her face up so she had to look at him.

'This is ridiculous,' she muttered, her eyes sliding away.

'No, I'm interested,' he said. 'I'd be grateful for your advice. I'm a novice at proposals.' He gave her a mischievous smile.

'I'm not surprised,' Sally said, unduly waspish with relief. For a moment she had thought she felt the fingers under her chin turn to iron.

There had been that unmistakable challenge earlier, she recalled uneasily. She tried to convince herself that it would be beneath his dignity but she was not entirely sure that Paul might not, even now, gather her up again and finish her education in one swift, devastating encounter. Notwithstanding the waiting Amanda and the dinner party for which he was already late, she thought.

He held her away from him, leaning back so he could look down into her face.

'So how would you expect to be proposed to, Sally Harrison?'

'I don't expect to be proposed to,' she said swiftly.

His eyes narrowed. 'Now that's interesting. A feminist who doesn't want marriage—or who does her own proposing?'

'That's my business,' Sally said despairingly. It hadn't had much effect last time.

Nor did it this time. He shrugged, the bare shoulders glistening. Sally swallowed and averted her eyes rapidly.

'All right. How would you like to be proposed to?'

Sally removed herself and stood up. 'I said I don't think it's any business of yours,' she said with emphasis, making for the door.

Paul laughed softly. 'Chicken,' he taunted, stretching his arms luxuriously above his head, so that his muscles rippled.

She sent him a look of dislike.

'I am not chicken. I just think it's private.'

'But I've asked you to marry me,' he pointed out. 'That's not private. And, somehow, I went wrong. You owe it to me to tell me where. Give me a hint on where my technique's let me down, darling.' And he gave her a melting look.

Sally decided not to hit him and to reply as if he were being serious. It should take the wind out of his sails, she thought, at least for a moment.

So she said gently, 'It's not a matter of technique. It's a matter of being right together. Of being in love.'

He propped himself up against the pillows as if he had all night to pursue the topic. And he looked interested enough to do it, too. His smile was lop-sided.

'Are you in love, then, Harrison?'

Sally crossed her fingers behind her back. 'No.'

He looked mournful. 'You're telling me I'm not the man of your dreams.'

'Yes, that's what I'm telling you,' Sally agreed, crossing her fingers harder.

'And what would he have done? The man of your dreams?' persisted Paul, looking intrigued.

Sally sighed.

'Come on, Harrison, give me a clue. Shower you with diamonds? Write sonnets to your eyebrow? Go down on one knee in the moonlight?'

His eyes were dancing. He obviously thought she was so dull that nobody would ever make a romantic gesture in her direction, Sally thought indignantly.

She glared at him. 'All of those. And more.'

He laughed out loud. '*More*?' He was incredulous.

'Much more,' said Sally firmly. 'He'd make me feel I was the only woman in the world. He'd make me feel *loved*.'

'You think I couldn't?' He was interested.

'Paul Theokaris, you are a rich, busy man with a nasty sense of humour,' she told him roundly. 'We have nothing in common. And you're out of my league. The only thing you make me feel is wary.'

Paul was still laughing when she walked out, banging the door behind her.

CHAPTER FOUR

SALLY fled the flat with all speed. She knew that Paul's dress shirt would not have survived uncreased and decided ruthlessly that it was Paul's problem. He had forced her into the position of rolling around on it. He could sort it out. She wasn't ironing it again.

She left the iron ostentatiously on the kitchen unit before she left.

When she got back to her office the telephone was ringing. She looked at it with dislike and switched on the answering tape. Whoever it was rang off as soon as the machine answered.

Sally smiled grimly to herself. Probably Paul, demanding she go back and fasten his cuff-links. Well, for once he'd have to manage on his own. It was probably, she thought as she let herself out, a record.

She had a long wait for the train, and an even longer one outside a suburban station once she got on it. So she arrived home in the dark with an admirable excuse for her temper. Andrew, after one crisp exchange about the state of his room, grabbed a hearty plate of Welsh rarebit and retired to do his homework. Gramps looked thoughtful.

'Job too much for you?' he asked at last.

Much of Sally's ire had cooled in the kitchen. Now she shook her head tiredly.

'It's not that.'

'Difficult to work for, is he? Theokaris?'

Her shoulders sagged. She tipped her head back against the elderly upholstery of the armchair.

'Not usually. Things aren't going well for him at the moment and—well, like the rest of us, he's not a saint,' she said carefully.

Gramps sent her a shrewd look.

'In other words, he's giving you hell. Only loyal secretaries don't tell.'

Sally shook her head, laughing a little. 'You know me too well.'

He frowned. 'I know you well enough to know you don't usually get yourself in this state for nothing.'

Sally jumped.

'And everything seemed well enough yesterday. When he brought you home. Very friendly, he was, I thought. Not a bad chap,' Gramps said in the tone of one making great concessions, 'in spite of all that money.' He shot her another searching look. 'So what happened today? It's not like you to go blasting poor old Andrew over a few dirty socks.'

Sally said nothing.

'Or was it something last night? You were a bit absent-minded this morning, but...' He leaned forward, taking in her expression. 'What is it, pet? Did Theokaris make a pass at you?' he said gently.

'Gramps!' Sally protested.

'What did he do?' said Grandfather, ignoring her protest. There was a distinctly militant air to him.

Sally patted his arm.

'Nothing terrible,' she assured him drily. She knew her grandfather's prejudices very well. He was quite convinced that the wealthy and aristocratic were waiting for any opportunity to oppress the working poor. 'He's not a vile seducer of dairymaids. At least,' she amended conscientiously, 'it would probably depend on the dairymaid. But he's not a vile seducer of secretaries.'

Except that only that evening the secretary in question had flung herself at him in a manner it was not in Paul

Theokaris's temperament to ignore. Sally had been struggling with that unwelcome realisation all the way home on the crawling train, and it had not got any easier to bear. God knew how she was going to face him in the morning.

She flushed and went on hurriedly, 'Actually, last night he was suggesting something rather different. He thought—well, his family are pushing him to marry and he thought we might . . . sort of merge.'

Her grandfather stared at her. Presumably he couldn't see what an international playboy, even a reformed one like Paul Theokaris, could see in her either, Sally thought.

Then he said unexpectedly, 'It might not be a bad thing at that.'

She repressed a superstitious shiver. Her grandfather didn't notice.

'Theokaris,' he said musingly. 'You could do worse. Got a lot of life about him.'

'Don't you mean he's got a lot of bank accounts about him?' Sally said coldly.

Her grandfather sat bolt upright and stared at her.

'Sally Harrison, you take that back. I've never thought money was important all my life and I'm not starting now. And you should know it.'

She subsided. 'Yes. Yes, I do know it. I'm sorry, Gramps.'

'That's not to say it wouldn't be helpful,' he added fair-mindedly. 'With Andrew growing and needing his chances. But the important thing is *you*. Why don't you want to marry him? Fine-looking man. Thought you were fond of him. Plenty of charm.'

'That's three reasons,' Sally said drily.

'So you *are* fond of him.' There was a pause before he said slowly, 'Sally, are you scared?'

'Of marrying Paul Theokaris? Terrified,' she said in a flippant tone. She didn't need to cross her fingers; it was the unvarnished truth.

Grandfather looked perturbed.

'You know, you need to see a bit more of life. You've run this house like a woman twice your age. But you're only a girl. Andrew won't need you at home forever and you can't spend your life looking after an old man. And that job of yours is fine but it's no career.'

Sally said nothing. He looked even more worried.

'Surely you want marriage and children, Sally? I know some girls don't, but not you. You were born for it.'

She moved restlessly. She debated. Perhaps she could tell him some, at least, of the truth.

'I don't think I'm the marrying type, Gramps. I've known that for years. It's got nothing to do with Paul. Or not really.'

She thought of her mother, doting and endlessly hurt; of her father, reduced to violent temper by the very affection he inspired. Paul Theokaris wasn't a violent man but he was a private one, for all his well-documented social frivolities. And he'd made it very clear he wasn't in love with her or anything like it. Whereas she—— Sally shuddered. He wouldn't want her love. It would embarrass him and worse. Marrying him would be the worst sort of trap.

She said carefully, 'I think people need more space than there's room for in most marriages. Or I do, anyway.'

Her grandfather watched her unblinkingly for a bit. Then he nodded his head as if he'd decided something.

'You *are* afraid.'

'I'm not much of a risk taker,' she corrected quietly. 'And marriage is an awful risk, Gramps.' She looked down at her hands. 'Especially if the—the feeling isn't equal on both sides.'

He nodded again but he didn't seem inclined to argue. 'So what are you going to do about Theokaris?'

She was so startled to be returned to the original subject of conversation that she blushed, deeply and un-disguisably. Gramps said nothing, but he could not fail to notice.

'Nothing,' Sally said sharply. 'It was only an idea. He'll forget about it soon enough. From the way he was behaving today, he's forgotten it already,' she added waspishly.

Except for when he held me in his arms and drove me quietly out of my mind. Except for when he called me a closet romantic. Except for... Stop it, she thought. Stop it. You don't want him, you can't handle him and you're playing with fire if you even let yourself think about it.

'He's got plenty of other things to think about at the moment, heaven knows.'

'Hmm,' said her grandfather.

But to her great relief he said no more.

Sally decided to clean the kitchen. She scrubbed and scoured and soaked and scraped until well after mid-night. There was a certain satisfaction in turning the homely kitchen into a sterile area but it did nothing for the embarrassing memories scurrying round in her brain.

She went to bed at half-past one. She got up at six-fifteen, exhausted and sleepless. Every time she turned over under her quilt, she heard his husky murmur or felt his hands on her skin as if he were there in the narrow bed with her.

'Damn him,' she said.

She made herself a mug of hot chocolate, as her mother had done when she was a child and hurt herself. There was a little comfort in the warm sweetness. But it felt wrong, sitting at the table in the grey light of dawn, agonising over her body's shameful responses to a careless rake.

That's what he is, she told herself fiercely. Nothing but a rake. A rake with a nasty sense of humour.

But he asked you to marry him, a softer, gentler part of herself reminded her; the part that was thinking wistfully about what it would be like to have Paul Theokaris love and care for you.

Only because he knew you wouldn't get in the way of his adventures, said the Sally who didn't dream. You're plain and sensible and you know the score. He told you so.

He didn't say you were plain. He only said you were sensible, the optimist offered.

He didn't *need* to say I'm plain. We both know it. And sensible in his terms means someone who won't make a fuss, said the tougher Sally, uncomforted. It's not good enough.

He could pay for Andrew's trip to France. And if he went on to university...

The price, said sensible Sally, concluding the argument, is too high. If he mentions it again I shall tell him so. But the betting is he won't. Not after the exhibition I made of myself last night.

The thought of that exhibition so thoroughly unsettled her that she finished her hot chocolate and several months' mending before Andrew and Gramps were stirring.

In spite of her early night, or perhaps because of it, she was late at work. This was sufficiently unusual to cause the commissionaire to ask after her health as she passed through the vestibule.

'Fine, thank you,' she told him. 'The train was a little delayed.'

When she got up to her office, it was plain not only that Paul had arrived but also that his uncle was with him. Of course, she thought with a start. He had been to his breakfast meeting with the bankers this morning. From the volume coming from his office, it did not sound as if the meeting had gone too well.

'I told you,' Costas was roaring. 'I bloody *told* you.'

Paul's reply was indecipherable. Sally closed her ears to the tempest and went about unlocking the safe, readying her computer and going through the post. The intercom buzzed. She leaned forward, pressing the button.

'Yes?'

'Oh, you're in at last, are you?' said Paul disagreeably. 'Get in here. And bring your shorthand book.'

It did not sound as if he was going to raise the subject of marriage again, thought Sally, smiling in spite of herself.

'Very well, Mr Theokaris.'

She stood up, smoothed her slim black skirt, and went in.

'And you can stop Mr-Theokarising me,' Paul said from his seat at the window. 'I've had enough to bear today, heaven help me, without you adding your mite. Sit down and take that disapproving scowl off your face.'

Sally was startled. He was not normally rude to her—and never in front of anyone else. She sat down on the chair in front of the desk, nodding to Costas, who grunted a response.

'Very well,' she said quietly.

Costas said, 'Don't be a fool. Do what your stepmother wants, boy. Then she'll cough up. Damn it, it's not hard. It comes to all of us in time. And you've had your own way long enough. Blasted spoilt child,' said Costas, losing his conciliatory tone fast.

Paul leaned forward.

'Let me remind you I can walk away from the shambles you've made of this company any time I like,' he said evenly. 'If you want to sort it out—fine. I'll go to-morrow. Otherwise we do things my way.'

There was a pregnant silence. Costas turned on his heel and walked out.

Sally stayed resolutely silent. It was not often that she forgot herself enough to voice her feelings about his family. Paul was normally meticulous in his loyalty to them—which, in her private opinion, they didn't deserve.

Instead she said gently, 'I'll make some coffee.'

Paul didn't turn.

'You can be a pain, Harrison. But there are times when I think you're second cousin to the angels,' he said with an attempt at lightness. 'My bloodstream is definitely in need of a caffeine injection.'

She was making the coffee when the telephone rang again. It was Costas. She put him through to Paul at once. She was carefully prising open a carton of milk when she heard Paul's howl of rage. It was so out of character that she rushed into his office.

He was standing at the window with the handset in one hand. His face was a mask of anger.

'She can do what she damned well likes,' he said. It was a cold whisper, filled with such venom that it brought Sally up short. 'I don't care,' he added to some evident protest from Costas.

He cut off the call and flung the telephone away from him. In pure reflex action, Sally ran forward and caught it. He looked at her alarmed face. There was a long, pregnant minute while he clenched his fists and said nothing.

Then he said, 'Oh, hell, this is turning into a farce.'

And began to laugh.

Cautiously Sally returned the telephone to its place.

'Do you think I'm mad, Sally? I wouldn't blame you if you did.'

She said carefully, 'You're not behaving in character this morning. But then I don't know what provocation you've had.'

'Sensible Sally,' Paul said. 'I take it back. You're *first* cousin to the angels.' He sat down on the seat in front of the tall window and drew one leg up in front of him. 'I've had the provocation that would drive a man to murder, Sally. Multiple murder. My family is full of damned fools and hypochondriacs with a taste for bad melodrama. None of them has the sense he was born with. Or a conscience.'

Since three years of working for the Theokaris organisation had given Sally roughly the same impression, she made no reply other than an encouraging noise.

'My stepmother,' he said, 'has gone into hospital in Switzerland. She hasn't had a good meaty drama in her life for a couple of months, so she's decided she's dying. So she wants to see her little girl settled before she goes.' His voice was heavily ironic.

Light began to dawn on Sally.

'Stephanie?'

'As you say. The wondrous Stephanie. Now she has convinced her mother that she wants to marry *me*.'

'Good lord,' said Sally, awed.

'You may well say so,' he agreed. 'The trouble is that the Press have been making some copy about my not being a settled family man. They've been pointing out that I haven't been with the company since I left school and hinting that I might move back to my own consultancy full-time if the going gets rough. So Costas has already told me he thinks I should get married and establish my bona fides.'

'That's crazy,' said Sally involuntarily, forgetting her professional discretion.

'I didn't take it too seriously,' Paul agreed. 'Only Costas does. And somehow he's convinced my stepmother. At the moment she's the only one with the money to provide the capital injection we need if we're going to buy Costas's Japanese ship. So——' He shrugged expressively.

He tipped his head back against the alcove wall. His dark hair flopped over his forehead. He ran a hand through it impatiently.

Sally thought with a sudden lurch of her stomach: Stephanie. He's going to marry Stephanie. It was like a bucket of cold water over her head. She sat down abruptly. She found she was shivering as if from shock.

'Now that she's going into hospital, Anne's decided she'll put the money into the company. At a price. To secure her little girl's future, I've got to marry Stephanie within a month.' He snorted.

Sally said, 'Stephanie was here yesterday. She wanted to see you. I left a message.'

'She saw Costas last night. He's ordering the wedding cake.'

Sally thought she was going to be sick. Why do I care? she thought. He's not for me. He never was for me. Why do I feel as if I'm having my stomach pulled out through my throat?

'Congratulations,' she managed.

Paul turned his head and glared at her. She rose hastily.

'If you're trying to be funny, Harrison——'

The phone rang. This time it was the lawyer. Paul took the call eagerly. Sally left.

When she went back into the office with his coffee he was sitting in his swivel chair with his feet on the desk and a distinct gleam in his eyes. Paul Theokaris, she deduced, was fighting back. She made to retreat but he waved her into a chair.

'Say that again, Edward.'

He leaned forward and switched the machine to broadcast.

'A very dubious area of law. Of course, it would depend on the jurisdiction. If, however, you were already married, there would be no question of its being possible.'

'You mean, if I get married before she signs the damn thing I don't have to marry Stephanie *and* she'll take up the new shares anyway?'

Sally's heart clenched tight in her breast. *Not* marry Stephanie?

'It's probable.' The dry voice became slightly less lawyer-like. 'The truth is, if you're already married the old bat won't try it on. But you haven't got a lot of time, Paul. Nigel is flying out with the papers tomorrow. And you're not going to find a decent woman to take you on in twenty-four hours.'

'A decent woman,' Paul repeated thoughtfully.

His eyes gleamed at her. The ridiculously long eyelashes dropped, then lifted. He gave her a blazing smile.

'You're a decent woman, aren't you, Harrison?'

'What?' said the unseen Edward, confused.

'Hang on, Edward. A touch of in-house negotiation at this end.' He leaned forward. 'Well, my angel? Would you take me on at twenty-four hours' notice, decent woman that you are?'

Sally could have hit him. Instead she gave him a composed smile and said, 'I'm not a woman, decent or not. I'm a word processor and a personal organiser with total recall. So I don't count.'

Paul said, 'You'll have to do.' He said to the telephone briskly, 'Better get over here, Edward. We'll have one of those agreements of yours drawn up. And get me a marriage licence that does the deed before Nigel lets Anne sign the papers. Get him off tomorrow's plane. He can have a week's holiday anywhere in the world at my expense.'

There was outraged spluttering from the other end. Paul sat up very straight.

'Do it,' he said crisply. He cut the call.

Sally said almost in a shriek, 'Will you *stop* this?'

Paul got up and came towards her. His face was serious. The laughing eyes were sober for once.

'When I asked you to marry me you said we'd talk about it later,' he reminded her crisply. 'This is later.'

Sally closed her eyes. 'I thought it was a joke.'

'No, you didn't.' He sounded very cool, very much master of the situation; even faintly amused. But implacable. 'You were walking round me on eggshells all day yesterday in case I demanded my answer.'

So he'd noticed. He was altogether too clever. Sally opened her eyes and glared at him defiantly.

'I wasn't exactly walking round you last night,' she retorted with heat. And instantly regretted it.

The dark eyes gleamed. 'True. Rather encouraging on the whole. But you still weren't answering the big one.'

'Oh, yes, I was,' she said, blushing and furious with him because of it. 'I said no, in case you've forgotten.'

He waved an impatient hand. 'A little feminine evasion.'

'It wasn't. I told you——'

'Yes, I know. It wasn't the proposal of your dreams and I'm not the man to make you feel wanted. I haven't forgotten.'

Sally was surprised and showed it. The handsome mouth slanted wryly at her reaction.

'You don't give much away normally. When you do, I store it up for future use,' Paul told her coolly. 'I'm sorry young Lochinvar hasn't turned up. But I have. I'll have to see what I can do about fulfilling your fantasies later.' The teasing went out of his voice. He sounded crisp and practical all of a sudden. 'Look, Sally, you and I have both got problems. I think we could solve each other's. And mine are pressing.'

The matter-of-fact tone was quite chilling to Sally. It was the voice he used when negotiations were over and he was putting his plans into practice. She stood up slowly.

'I—will—not—marry—you,' she said clearly.

Paul was unmoved. 'I don't think you have a lot of choice. There's no point in being stubborn.'

She gasped. 'What do I have to do...? Wouldn't you be stubborn, in my place?'

'Probably,' he said, surprising her. He dismissed it with a quick, almost angry movement. 'It's not important. We have to think about what we do next.'

Sally drew a long, steadying breath and grasped the back of the chair with a firm hand. She needed the support.

'What I'm going to do next is get you a substitute secretary from the pool, finish the post and go home,' she said with deliberation. 'I don't like this nonsense and I won't put up with it.'

Paul gave her a measuring look.

'You're not very polite. I've never asked a woman to marry me before.'

'You haven't *asked* me,' flashed Sally, lifting her head. 'You've told me.'

Paul considered it.

'That's fair,' he admitted at last. 'I'll apologise if you like.'

'Thank you,' she said drily.

'But you must see the extenuating circumstances,' he went on as if she hadn't spoken. 'This is an emergency.'

Sally's temper went to white heat. Presumably it was the reaction to shock, she told herself. She tried not to remember that the worst shock had been thinking that he was going to marry Stephanie.

'Not for me.'

His mouth tightened.

'Oh, yes, it is, Sally. We are talking corporate survival here. You're bright enough to know that.'

'That's nothing to do with me,' she retorted.

'You'll get a job this well paid easily?' he asked politely. 'At the drop of a hat? Without having to wait between jobs?'

'I'm a first-class secretary,' she hissed.

'Oh, agreed. I'll write the reference. But...'

She paled. 'You wouldn't give me a bad one out of spite?'

For a moment his eyes flared and she thought she had really angered him. Then he said quietly, 'No, I wouldn't do that.'

'Then I'll get another job.'

'Yes,' he agreed. 'Eventually. But I've seen the way you live, Sally. I've talked to your grandfather. He needs an operation on his eyes. You didn't know that, did you? You can't afford it. I'm paying you well and you *still* can't cope financially. Not really. Can you?'

It was true. Sally stared at him. The fight began to drain out of her as she thought of the bills, the rewiring, Andrew's school trip... And what was he saying about Gramps's eyes?

She said sharply, 'What sort of operation?'

'He's got a cataract. The hospital tell him that he'll be operated on in two years. But it's got so much worse in the last four months that he's afraid he'll be virtually blind before he gets to the top of the queue,' Paul told her quietly.

'He never said a word about it to me. You're making it up,' she flung at him. 'Why would he tell you?'

Paul shrugged. 'Because I had time to listen?'

Sally winced. 'I don't believe you,' she said. 'I'd have noticed something.'

She suddenly remembered Gramps's reluctance to go out. She'd noticed that. She just hadn't drawn the right conclusions, it seemed. She bit her lip.

He saw the doubt in her face and followed his advantage through ruthlessly. It was typical. Sally recognised the practised deal-maker at work even as the full force of his words began to sink in. She resented it but she couldn't prevent her instinctive reactions.

'Look,' he said, 'money will solve all your problems. I've got it. You said yourself you ought to make me send the kid brother round the world——'

'It was a joke...' she said faintly.

He ignored the interruption.

'—and that house is falling down. Your grandfather's been told he's got to wait two years to have his cataracts removed under the National Health. Can he afford to wait two years? How long before he's completely blind and can't go out of the house on his own?'

The words beat at her like physical blows. She thought of Gramps not being able to get to the allotments to see his friends there. He would hate being caged in the house.

Shaken, she said, 'He didn't tell me.'

'Because he thinks you've got enough to worry about already,' Paul said swiftly. 'He told me.'

Sally stared at him. 'Why? Why you?'

He hesitated; then looked away, shrugging. 'Who knows? It's not important. The important thing is, he can have the operation next week if somebody picks up the tab. I will. But would you let me if I weren't a member of the family?'

Sally sat down rather abruptly. Her eyes seemed to blur. She didn't even ask how much it would cost. She knew it would be way beyond her present means. She felt helpless.

'Why are you doing this?' she said at last in an exhausted voice.

He didn't give her a direct answer. Instead he said harshly and unexpectedly, 'Sally, stop daydreaming. Young Lochinvar isn't going to turn up out of nowhere. And, if he did, he couldn't pay your bills.'

She gave a little jump. The room came back into focus. Paul dropped on one knee beside her chair.

'A bargain,' he said. 'That's what I'm offering. A fair exchange. You marry me and I can get Anne to invest without having the appalling Stephanie round my neck. In return I'll set up a trust for your family—medical bills, educational bills, whatever you want. You get the security you need and I get what I need.'

'All you need is camouflage,' Sally interrupted bitterly. 'Probably not for very long, either.'

Paul looked down at her ringless hand and stroked it. Sally stiffened, wrenching it away.

'Don't worry about that. I've got Edward drawing up one of these pre-nuptial contracts. I'll make sure you're comfortable when—if—we part.'

Sally winced. 'What forethought,' she mocked, though it hurt surprisingly sharply. It couldn't have been more obvious that his heart was not engaged at all.

'Forethought and planning. The secret of success,' Paul said smugly. 'Come on, face up to it, Sally. What else can you do?'

It was sufficiently true to make her want to strike out. She searched his face. What she saw made her realise two things with icy clarity: he liked her, but he wouldn't fall in love with her in a million years; and he was absolutely determined to marry her. The last hit her with the force of an earth-mover. Her resistance shattered.

'I give up. You win. You'll probably regret this and so shall I, but I'll do whatever you want,' she said, her fury none the less obvious for being repressed.

He seemed to freeze, almost as if she had surprised him, which couldn't have been true. Paul Theokaris was used to getting what he wanted. Or as if she'd hurt him; which was ridiculous. Then he sat back on his heels and grinned at her.

'No, you won't regret it. I'll see you don't,' he said confidently.

To her utter astonishment, he raised her hand to his lips, like an eighteenth-century courtier, and kissed it. Sally's world tilted. Her anger sank out of sight and for a crazy moment she felt more cared-for than she had ever been in her life.

He's not emotionally involved, she reminded herself frantically. This is just window dressing. Don't build anything on it. Tears started. She rapidly lowered her lashes, so he shouldn't see.

Paul stood up and smiled down at her. Now that he'd got his own way, he looked almost tender.

But she was still wrapped in that deceptive sensation of being cherished. In spite of her reservations, Sally smiled back shyly. She realised, with a little shock, that she was not only infatuated with this man—which, of course, he must never know—but that she would trust him with her life. As, indeed, she was going to do.

In retrospect, Sally realised that that was her second and worst mistake.

CHAPTER FIVE

SALLY went through the next seventy-two hours in a daze. For the first time she had the full blast of Paul's formidable energy channelled in her direction, and it was a formative experience.

'The trouble with you,' she told him faintly, 'is that you have the habit of command. It's tough on the ones you're commanding.'

He grinned at her.

'Close your eyes and go with the flow. I know what I'm doing.'

'I hope for all our sakes you do,' she said. 'Because I'm out of orbit. I'm just not making sense any more.'

'Makes a nice change,' he said unsympathetically. 'Very restful. Stick with it.'

Sally laughed, as he had intended, but the truth was that she did indeed feel as if she had had all will-power and initiative drained out of her. It was rather alarming. She had never behaved like it before in all her well-conducted life. She did what he said, when he said. Like a little automaton, she thought in disgust.

Her grandfather, noticing it, expressed surprise and disapproval. It was the only thing on which he did.

It surprised her. If she was honest, it disappointed her. Even while she was agreeing to Paul's suggestion, Sally had half expected opposition from her family. But Grandfather, though he dismissed with a wave her anxious enquiries about the cataract operation, seemed oddly relieved about her announcement. So her expected alibi for ducking out did not materialise.

Her grandfather, ignoring Paul's filthy riches and handmade shoes alike, took him off to the allotments for a man-to-man talk. It went on, it seemed to a jumpy Sally, for hours, and when they came back Gramps seemed quietly satisfied. It left Paul thoughtful.

Andrew, one calculating eye on the Jaguar, was frankly delighted.

They were both only too willing to fall in with Paul's lordly announcement that the wedding would be in three days' time. In fact, a Monday afternoon off school would have been enough on its own to convince Andrew that his new brother-in-law was an ace acquisition, as Sally pointed out acidly.

Paul was smug. 'One likes to get off on the right foot. I thought it would cost me a fortune in discs and designer clothes, but he seems as indifferent to worldly goods as his sister.'

'Thank you,' said the sister in question awfully. 'What you mean is he's an idle little toad and you're going to encourage him to curry favour.'

Paul looked rueful. 'I need an ally,' he agreed. 'Andrew gives me hope.'

'I don't know what you're talking about.'

'No, you probably don't.'

They were sitting in the tiny Harrison dining-room with a series of lists of pre-wedding essential activities in front of them. Paul looked at her curiously.

'They're very fond of you.'

She stared. 'Well, of course. It's mutual.'

'Yes, I can see that.' He shuffled the lists in his hands, looking down at them. A curious smile, part rueful, part sad, played about his mouth. 'It's not what I'm used to. I don't think there are two members of the Theokaris family who can stay in the same room together without fighting.'

Sally chuckled in spite of herself. 'You and Costas don't always fight,' she demurred.

'Costas and I are the exception. I've always had a lot of sympathy for him. Which,' he added grimly, 'I'm reconsidering. He got us into this mess.'

'Yes,' said Sally, her sparkle dying.

The sense of unreality got worse. The trouble was that nobody but herself seemed to have any sense that there was anything extraordinary happening. The Harrison family adjusted in minutes; Andrew's school accepted without comment the news that he could now go on the study tour to France; and even Paul's lawyer had arrived with a briefcase full of agreements, trust deeds and settlements. He showed absolutely no astonishment, to Sally's surprise. He even congratulated her in an absent-minded way. They were all mad, Sally thought a little hysterically.

Jane Drummond was the maddest of the lot.

Taken into their confidence with instructions from Paul to find Sally something pretty to get married in, she gasped, got her second wind and swept Sally out into Costas's chauffeur-driven car to the West End boutiques that the Cornelius women patronised.

'It's wonderful,' Jane said, her eyes shining. 'Of course, I knew he was crazy about you. But you're always so cool. I didn't think he'd get anywhere.'

Sally sent her one incredulous look and then firmly changed the subject. It was clear that Jane's romantic heart was busy rewriting history, she thought. But Jane wasn't having the subject changed.

'I'm so *glad*. You deserve a break. And he's so nice,' said Jane. 'Terribly glamorous, of course. But he looks like the sort of person you could talk to, as well.'

'Yes,' Sally agreed, surprised at Jane's perception. He was a man you could talk to and she had. For no reason at all, there was a lump in her throat.

It was still there when they got to the boutique. While Jane plucked dresses off hangers and paraded happily, Sally was fighting hard to hold on to a sense of reality.

This, she thought, is ridiculous. But she had a dark feeling that somehow the small ceremonies were tying her harder and harder to the unreality of being Paul's wife. It didn't make it any more real. But it did make it more alarming.

Jane found the perfect wedding dress, a full-length sweep of figured cream brocade with a pointed waist and ivory embroidery at the hem.

'Look,' she said, enraptured.

'Don't be ridiculous,' Sally said sharply. 'I'd look like the ugly sister pretending to be a princess out of a pantomime. I need something neat and practical I can wear afterwards.'

Jane's eyebrows rose. 'That's not what Paul said.'

'Paul knows nothing about it. It's my dress.'

'Well, he told me to make sure you didn't buy a business suit,' Jane retorted, revealing a conspiracy that Sally had not suspected. She looked at the lovely gown fondly. 'I think Paul would like that.'

'Very probably. But not on me,' said Sally. She turned to the sales assistants, who were looking carefully uninterested. 'I want a smart, plain suit. Nothing ostentatious.'

Jane sighed. But she joined in good-naturedly. In the end Sally bought a dress and jacket in leaf-green with russet trimmings.

'It's too old for you,' said Jane, sighing. 'But it's pretty. It does things for your hair. You need emeralds with it, I think.'

They were going towards the car, where Costas's chauffeur was holding the door open respectfully. Sally stopped dead and rounded on Jane.

'You are *not* to tell him that.'

Jane looked astonished at her tone.

'Whyever not?'

'I don't want him loading me with jewellery boxes like some, some . . .'

'Fiancée?' suggested Jane, amused.

Sally groaned.

'Like one of his playmates,' she snapped. 'Promise me you won't say anything to him about my wanting emeralds.'

'I won't,' Jane soothed, easing her into the car and nodding to the driver. 'I couldn't,' she added with a chuckle, 'as you obviously don't. But aren't you being a bit unrealistic? I mean, I know this is all a big rush, but Paul's going to want to do it properly.'

Sally didn't answer. It was a reflection that was occurring to her all too often in the middle of all this unreality. If Paul was bent on making the marriage a thorough production with all the special effects, she thought wryly, she was going to be out of her depth very soon.

She did not know what Paul had in mind for after the wedding, once his immediate problem was solved. He wouldn't stop still long enough to discuss it. All he did was snap out orders as he dashed past. But that unwillingness to talk was making Sally very uneasy indeed.

Jane said comfortably, 'Wedding nerves.'

Sally took a grip on herself. 'You're probably right.'

'It'll all be over by Monday night. Then you can look back on this and laugh.'

'Yes,' said Sally hollowly. She had a nasty feeling she was never going to laugh again.

She did not know what Jane reported to Paul. He gave her an odd look when she got back to the office. But she was too intent on bringing her work up to date and he was too involved with the finance director and a couple of bankers for them to exchange more than a few trivial words.

When the bankers left he came out to her. He stood in front of her desk and smiled down at her.

'Do you realise, I've never taken you out? Don't you think it's time I bought you dinner?'

Sally jumped and shook her head. She said quickly, 'The diary is full.'

She would not look at him. Paul stared down at her, exasperated.

'With dates I'm not going to keep. Don't be stupid, Sally. There's too much to do.'

She did look up then.

'Then you haven't got the time to take me to dinner.'

His eyes narrowed. 'Don't you think we need some time together?'

'We see each other all day.'

'Quality time,' he said patiently.

She swallowed. 'We'll have plenty of that after we're married.'

'Will we?' His voice was dry. 'You relieve my mind. I thought you were intending to carry on living in Bromley and seeing me in the office.'

She met his eyes. They were unreadable. She had been worrying about what happened next and now he seemed willing to discuss it. Illogically, Sally went into full retreat.

'The bargain was that I marry you. Not that I change homes,' she said pleasantly.

Paul bent forward and put his hands on her desk.

'On Monday evening,' he said deliberately, 'you're coming back with me to my flat. Or wherever.'

Sally was aghast. 'But Andrew, Gramps...'

'There won't be room for them in the flat,' Paul agreed. 'That's why I said we need to have some time together. There are one or two logistical problems that need straightening out. Eventually. But on Monday evening after our wedding you and I are spending the night, to say nothing of the ensuing days, at home. Together. Do I make myself clear?'

Sally had the familiar, unpleasant sensation of a bucket of water having been dropped over her head.

'But—why?'

Paul's face became grim. 'Because I don't play games.'

Sally drew an uncertain breath. 'I don't understand,' she complained.

'No, I'm beginning to realise that,' Paul said wryly.

She looked up at him pleadingly.

'Look, the lawyers will tell Mrs Theokaris we're married. Surely it won't matter to her whether I—er—move in with you or not. She needn't know.'

'I'll know,' said Paul unanswerably. 'And it matters to me.'

'You're impossible,' Sally muttered.

'I would have hoped,' he added acidly, 'that it would matter to you.'

Sally leaned forward and glared at him. 'I wish you'd make up your mind whether this is a practical bargain or a French farce,' she told him. 'If you wanted someone to move in with you, heaven knows there were plenty of candidates.'

Paul gave a choke of laughter. 'Well, if I ever thought I was irresistible, I've learned my lesson. Can't you just accept that I'd like to take you out for dinner?'

'You never have before,' pointed out Sally unanswerably. 'And I want to go home to look after my family.'

His eyes narrowed. 'Hiding behind them, Sally? You know, they won't thank you for being possessive.'

He paused. Sally preserved a determined silence. He sighed.

'Oh, have it your own way. Not tonight. I'll drive down tomorrow and take you out to lunch.'

It wasn't a success. For one thing, he arrived before Sally was ready, to find her still in stained jeans and an old cricket shirt of Andrew's. Paul's casual clothes were bought in New York and worn, or so Sally suspected, on yachts in the Mediterranean. His look of shock at her paint-stained jeans confirmed it. For another, she was in a vile mood.

She snapped all the way to the riverside pub. She couldn't make up her mind what she wanted to eat. And, when she finally chose and it came, Sally found she couldn't manage more than a couple of mouthfuls. That she was thoroughly ashamed of herself made her all the more combative.

Paul bore it with equanimity. 'You're thoroughly ratty,' he said kindly. 'Bad night?'

Since she had hardly slept, she could honestly have claimed that justification. But she was in a captious mood.

'Ordinary night. This is my normal self. You said you wanted to marry it,' she retorted.

He laughed. 'And, if you're thinking of frightening me into changing my mind, forget it. We have a date at the altar the day after tomorrow.'

Sally looked at him with a dislike which did not bode well for their marital contentment.

'And that's another thing—why can't you have a perfectly good register-office wedding? All this dashing about exhuming old college friends in holy orders is a waste of time.'

'It's my time,' he said mildly. 'I wouldn't feel married otherwise. Would you?'

Sally glared. 'I won't feel married anyway. Any more than I feel engaged.'

Paul looked amused. His eyebrows rose. 'You will,' he said softly. 'I've promised to look into the Lochinvar syndrome when I've got time.'

Her temper hit boiling-point.

'Don't laugh at me. Don't look at me like that. Stop pretending we're engaged like real people. You've just temporarily taken me over,' she spat.

He shook his head, his eyes dancing. 'You'll find you're wrong, I think.'

Sally looked about for something to throw. Then she realised that they were attracting a good deal of attention from other diners, sitting at the pretty waterside tables. She subsided. It was infuriating. He did not seem in the least annoyed by her behaviour. It seemed to entertain him.

She accompanied him silently back to the car and watched without interest as they twisted and turned through country lanes. It was only when he turned off the metalled highway on to a shingled drive that Sally even noticed they were not going home.

She sat up. 'Where——?'

He sent her a quick glinting look. 'Wait.'

The path wound through trees that seemed to get closer and closer. The path narrowed too. They were obviously going deep into a wood of some sort. Sally looked round uneasily.

It was beautiful. But it was very dense. The oak and birch were so close together that the sun broke through in individual bars of diamond light, slashing through the leaves like a sword.

When Paul stopped the car and the engine died away there was not a sound, apart from the chirrup of birds above them.

'Where are we?' Sally was angry to find herself whispering. 'Why have you brought me here?'

'In the middle of a deep, dark forest,' Paul said in thrilling tones. 'And I'm going to eat you up.'

Sally gave him a wry look, thinking of the last week. 'You mean you haven't already?'

He laughed. 'I haven't even started,' he said.

She eyed him uneasily, but he was opening his door and getting out.

'Come on. I want to show you something.'

She complied. It was not difficult walking. There was a path of sorts. It was covered with moss, which was slippery after the rain, and occasionally Paul had to hold back a briar for her to pass, but they went at a fairly good pace until they came to a clearing.

They were at the top of the hill. Ahead of them, the landscape of tree and hedge and pocket-handkerchief fields drowsed in the afternoon sun. The shadows were lengthening. The shadow of a hot-air balloon drifted across a distant field of corn.

Her temper dissolved like dawn mist.

'You can almost *smell* the peace,' Sally said, awed.

Paul looked pleased. She turned to him impulsively.

'Where is this place? Is it famous? I've never been here before.'

'It's part of an estate. The house—Galliards, it's called—is Victorian sub-Palladian, which is probably hell to heat. But at least it isn't too big, I thought,' he was casual, 'we might buy it. If you liked it.'

She did not understand at once.

'Theokaris Lines? Why? I thought the board rejected the conference-centre project. You said——'

'Not the company. Us. You and me,' Paul said with commendable patience.

There was a silence in which she could almost hear the air hum.

'Oh,' said Sally, enlightened. She felt as if she were in a lift which had suddenly broken free of its cable.

Paul said nothing. She darted a look at him. He was standing with his hands in his pockets, looking out over the valley. He looked calm and unanxious. You would not have thought he had just lobbed a bomb into the quiet atmosphere.

She said slowly, 'You're serious about this, aren't you?'

'Buying the house? Only if you like it.'

'No. I mean ...' Sally struggled to find the words for what she did mean. 'Marriage. Life after the wedding. Me.'

Paul turned to her. He was still calm but his eyes glinted in a way that meant he was at his most dangerous. Sally, who had watched him negotiate, knew.

'Of course.'

'But——'

'Did I ever say anything to make you think otherwise?'

Sally tried to pass their conversations on the subject under review. But her heart was hammering too hard. All her brain could grasp was the steady little flame in Paul's eyes and the determined set of his mouth.

'Oh, lord,' she said on a shaky little breath.

He did not touch her.

'You knew I was looking for a wife. I'd already told you I thought you and I had something going for us.'

'I thought you were just winding me up,' Sally confessed. 'I mean, we have so little in common.'

'Have we?'

'You have all that money. It's crazy. You're not in touch with the real world. Not my world. I don't know anything about the things you like—sailing and skiing and polo and—and I don't know how to dress or wear jewels. Your girlfriends are so sophisticated. I even wash my own hair,' she said not very coherently. The fervour was unmistakable, however.

Paul's eyes were shadowed.

'All that's important?'

She ignored that. 'All your girlfriends——'

Paul interrupted. '*That's* the problem, isn't it? You've got me down as some sort of playboy of the western world and you won't let the image go.'

Sally drew herself up to her full height.

'It's hardly an unjustified image,' she said coldly.

Paul took a quick step towards her. Her head went back. All the temper that had been simmering before came whooshing back. How dared he look so impatient, so *superior*?

'Can't you see——?'

It was Sally's turn to interrupt.

'I have been your secretary for four years,' she reminded him with heat. 'I know what's newspaper image and what's true. And that list of diamond-studded girlfriends is *true.*'

She turned her back on him, fighting the tears that, inexplicably, seemed about to overwhelm her. It was, she assured herself, pure anger.

'Sally!' Paul too sounded angry now, angry and peremptory. He put his hands on her shoulders and forced her round to face him. 'They knew the score. You *know* I never got serious about any one of them and they never got serious about me. I took good care of that.'

Just as he thinks he's taken good care that I don't get serious about him either, thought Sally bleakly. At least emotionally. Like my father, he doesn't want to be loved. It would tie him down. And he doesn't want the ties of a relationship with no escape route either.

Signing the lawyers' papers had shaken her badly with their implicit assumption that sooner or later Paul would go on his way. Leaving her and her family well provided-for, of course. Leaving them lavishly provided-for. It had hurt enough to make her gasp aloud in surprise, like a blow on a bruise.

Paul Theokaris was marrying her because she was a plain, sensible girl who wouldn't gíve him any trouble, Sally reminded herself. Because she was poor and needed his money without the complications of needing his love and support as well. And because he trusted her to accept the eventual, inevitable pay-off with good grace.

Only I *do* want his support, thought Sally wretchedly. I *do* want his love. Quite as much as any of those girlfriends that he's running away from. I'm not half as sensible as he thinks I am.

'I may have partied a bit when I was a youth,' Paul was saying drily. 'Though the papers made it sound more exciting than it felt. It was a long time ago. Fifteen years or more.' He touched her cheek very gently and said in a surprised voice, 'You're crying.'

'Temper,' Sally assured him swiftly, backing out of reach. 'Fifteen years, rubbish. And if you think the girlfriends I've met didn't get serious about you you're even more out of touch with the real world than I thought.'

Paul's mouth was wry. 'Serious about my money, maybe.'

'You're crazy.'

Suddenly his eyes flared. 'I must be, trying to talk sense into you. There's only one thing you understand, isn't there?'

Sally began to say, 'What do you mean?' when it became all too obvious what he meant.

It was not a kiss, it was an assault. He seemed to have no sense at all that what he held in his hands was a person, Sally thought. His mouth ravaged hers painfully. Her jaw felt as if it had been wrenched apart. There was the taste of blood on her tongue.

Suddenly Sally was frightened in a new way. There were too many echoes there, echoes of violence and pleading and unreason.

Sally tried to steady herself, reaching for cool reason. Paul wasn't really like her father, she reminded herself. Oh, he was dictatorial and demanding and he made sure he got his own way. But he wasn't violent and there was always that saving glint of humour.

Except that now the humour was gone. And he was using his strength on her in a way she had never experienced before; never even imagined. The fact that something buried deep inside her responded to it only made it the more alarming.

Sally tried to tear herself out of his grip, but he hardly seemed to notice. He loured over her, swamping her senses, overwhelming her. His strength was frightening. That too had echoes.

She dragged her mouth away.

'Please...' It was voiceless with shock.

Paul did not seem to hear. Sally pulled hard, bending away from him in an agonised arc until she thought her spine would crack. If he let her go now she would collapse in an ignominious heap on the moss. But Paul was exploring the long exposed curve of her throat. His hands were like iron at her back. Sally moaned.

Then suddenly he was letting her fall. Her knees buckled. She grabbed instinctively at his shoulders. He gave a soft laugh that turned her blood to ice. And she found herself being lowered to the forest floor. She flung herself sideways but he was too quick for her, pinning her with a hand on either side of her fallen body as he bent over her.

'You want serious?' he said, half under his breath.

Sally could hardly make her voice work. But she was desperate.

'Don't *touch* me,' she said in a voice raw with panic.

Paul froze.

Sally pushed him away and struggled into a sitting position. Twigs cracked under her hands as she did so.

She put the back of her hand to her sore mouth, wincing. Inside she was shaking uncontrollably. But for some reason it did not seem to show. The hand was steady.

She swallowed. Her heart slowed from its frantic tumbling. She was very cold. She brought her knees up and hunched behind them, clasping her arms round them protectively.

Paul was on one knee beside her. She couldn't look at him.

At last he said in a disbelieving voice, 'Sally?'

She kept her eyes stubbornly lowered.

'Sally, look at me.'

Paul bent forward and brought her chin up very gently. She had the feeling that he was moving carefully, as if the last few minutes had shocked him too.

'My dear——'

Had he ever called her that before? He had called her Harrison and Sensible Sally, and sometimes a drawling, sexy 'darling' that he knew she disapproved of. But 'my dear'? It sounded like what he would call a maiden aunt.

'Sally, stop cowering like that,' he said in a steady tone. 'I'm not going to hurt you. How can you think I would?'

'You didn't *listen* to me,' she muttered.

He did not say anything for a moment. Then he eased himself down on the moss and twigs and several seasons' dead leaves. He sat very close, facing her, his long legs bent. He was looking intently into her face. But he did not touch her.

Eventually he said, picking his words, 'I've kissed you before.'

Sally winced. Yes, he had kissed her and she had nearly floated off on a rosy haze of desire. She had not felt cold and excited and hungry. And frightened of the hunger.

He said in an odd voice, 'Why did you agree to marry me, Sally?'

She looked up then. Bewildered, she said, 'But you know...'

His expression didn't tell her much. And it didn't change.

'Remind me.'

Sally felt a flash of indignation. For a man who had pushed and bullied and played on her feelings as if she were a musical instrument, he was in no position to ask a question like that, she thought. Unless he thought it would be amusing to make her fall in love with him as well. Perhaps he wanted nothing less than total surrender. It was not a comforting thought.

She said more coolly, 'We had a bargain. Your money for my good sense.' In spite of her determination to remain unmoved, the words bit.

The dark eyes narrowed. He looked at her for a long moment and, to her shame, her whole body quickened.

Paul said softly, 'If you're waiting for me to promise not to make love to you, you'll wait forever.'

Sally set her teeth. She was tempted to give vent to the rage that she felt building inside her. The only thing that held her back was the thought that to a man of Paul's perception it would be altogether too revealing.

So she said sweetly, 'With a track record like yours, I would never have expected it.'

His brows flew up. She thought for a moment that his mouth twitched.

'Worried about other women, Sally? You've no need.'

'No,' she agreed. 'You're not marrying them.'

Because you wouldn't let anyone you were really attracted to get close enough to put chains on you. By marrying me, you're insuring your freedom. I won't have any more influence on you after we're married than I have now. And when you decide it's over, you think I'll go quietly. And you're probably right.

Sally realised it with a little shock. She hadn't put it to herself like that before.

'I'm glad you realise that,' Paul said softly. The dark eyes were watchful.

Sally said with difficulty, 'I can't——'

'Pretend to be in love with me,' Paul finished for her swiftly. 'I know. I never asked you to.'

Sally shut her eyes. The irony of it would have been funny if she hadn't been so miserable. She had no need to pretend to be in love with him. She had been besotted with him for months, maybe years. The only pretence involved had been in keeping it hidden.

'You don't understand.'

'No,' Paul said gently. '*You* don't understand.'

And he leaned forward and placed his lips softly against the corner of her mouth. Sally sat very still.

'There,' he said. 'Progress. You didn't run screaming into the undergrowth.'

She opened her mouth, found she had nothing to say and shut it again. He unclasped her hands and took one, unresisting, into his own warm palm. He closed the other over it, stroking her fingers with moth-wing strokes that made her skin shiver with pleasure. Sally looked hurriedly away.

'We're adults,' he said calmly. 'We've both got a lot to gain from this marriage. What we need is a bit of goodwill on both sides. A bit of forbearance. And time.'

The hypnotic fingers stilled.

'I won't give you any promises I can't keep, Sally. But I will give you time. Believe me.'

Paul sat back. He clearly felt he had presented an unassailable case. Sally looked at him doubtfully.

He sounded so sincere, she thought. He hadn't told her any lies. Or at least she thought he hadn't. He was a masterly manipulator of other people, of course; but she thought in this case he was honest. And all the practical reasons she had originally given herself for agreeing were still there. And all the reasons why it was going to tear her to pieces, too.

'I wish I knew what to *do*.' She drummed her fists on her knees.

'Trust me,' Paul said firmly.

Sally gave up. He wanted her to marry him. Her family wanted her to marry him. And in her deepest heart she wanted it too. Heaven help her. With enemies like those on the other side, she didn't have a chance.

CHAPTER SIX

MONDAY morning dawned cold and windy. Sally was awake before it was light. At half-past five she gave up the attempt to sleep and got up.

The kitchen was icy. She put on the kettle, as much to warm the atmosphere as to make a coffee she didn't want. Nobody was stirring. She had never felt so alone.

She took her cooling coffee into the front room and sat at the window. A few cars passed, going illegally fast down the empty street. When they had gone the silence felt like the end of the world.

What am I doing? Sally thought. I'll never be able to come back. After today everything will change and I don't know what it'll change into. Or what I'll change into. But I know this is over. It's been my life for more than ten years and it's over. And all because of a man who doesn't even *see* me properly. And he tells me to trust him.

She had no answers. She hadn't had any yesterday or last night, so it wasn't really a surprise. She wasn't fool enough to think that living with Paul would be bliss because she was in love with him, she thought. Loving him only made her more vulnerable to that terrible indifference.

Oh, he was charming. He had been born charming and he used it without thinking. Even on his secretary, sometimes. But she couldn't pretend that there was any real feeling there for her or any of his other girlfriends.

It felt like feeling, of course. Sally leaned forward and rested her tired brow against the window-pane. In his arms, with his mouth searching out her every secret, it felt so damned close to feeling that she had all too nearly succumbed. Turned to him. Begged him for love. Sally winced, remembering.

That mustn't happen again, she told herself. Though how she was going to hide her feelings for him when they were married she could not imagine. Especially if he wanted to make love to her. When he wanted to make love to her. He hadn't lied about that. She had a breathing-space but she didn't have forever. Somehow she was going to have to find a way of protecting her heart from all that careless charm and passion.

'Strictly limited passion,' Sally said out loud fiercely. 'Never forget that. He may want you. But he hasn't said he loves you. And he won't. Because he's honest.'

Trying to congratulate herself on Paul's honesty, she drained the nasty coffee and went to prepare herself.

That was why, when Grandfather came downstairs, intending to make her a breakfast tray and carry it up to her room, he found Sally scrubbing the kitchen floor and the air redolent of bleach and disinfectant. He stopped dead, blinking.

'If you and Andrew are going to be here on your own,' Sally said defensively to the unspoken question, 'I thought I'd leave it in a reasonable state.'

Grandfather looked round at gleaming tins and sparkling work surfaces and said a little faintly that he was very grateful to her. But hadn't she better, perhaps, get rid of the smell that hung about her person before she walked down the aisle to Paul?

'Oh, it's ages yet,' said Sally, her heart beating hard enough to remind her that it wasn't nearly long enough. 'I'll help you and Andrew first.'

Which was also why, when Jane Drummond arrived in the chauffeur-driven limousine to take her to Oxford for the ceremony, Sally was standing at the ironing-board, ruthlessly spraying starch on Andrew's shirt collar. Andrew and Gramps were watching her with expressions between horror and disbelief.

Jane summed up the situation in a glance.

'They'll look wonderful,' she said, taking the iron from Sally's hand. 'I'll finish here. You go and get your suitcase.'

'I'm not taking a suitcase,' said Sally, surrendering the task reluctantly. 'We're not staying, you know.'

Jane looked momentarily disconcerted. Then she attacked the shirt with a will.

'Well, you surely aren't going to wear your wedding outfit all the way down in the car,' she said over her shoulder. 'It'll get terribly creased. I'm sure Paul's expecting you to change. Anyway, he had me book a room at the Randolph so you could. *I*,' she added, clinching it, 'am going to.'

Sally sighed. 'Is it really necessary?'

Jane looked shocked. 'You want to look your best, don't you?' She did not wait for an answer. It was manifest that Sally didn't want to look her best. 'And there'll be flowers and things,' she added vaguely. 'Much better to get into your glad rags when we get there.'

Sally shrugged. It hadn't occurred to her, but she didn't really care. In fact it was probably better to spend the last tense minutes before she finally committed herself by climbing into the new dress instead of biting her fingernails, she thought wryly. Not that she could tell Jane that.

Jane supervised her packing with tremendous speed and hurried her into the car.

'What about your hair?' she said when they were settled. 'Have you arranged a hairdresser in Oxford?'

Sally shook her head. 'I don't know any hairdressers in Oxford. And, anyway, I do my own hair.'

Jane sat back in the corner of the luxurious leather seating and regarded her with pity.

'I don't understand you, Sally. Here you are, walking off with one of the world's prizes, and you act as if you're fitting him in between the supermarket and the eight-thirty to Waterloo.'

In the mirror Sally could see Costas's chauffeur grin. She knew him well enough to know that their conversation would be reported to Costas at the first opportunity. She frowned meaningfully at Jane.

But Jane was oblivious.

'They always used to say at college that we had to get the romance out of our systems. There was no such thing as a kind considerate boss who was also tall, dark and handsome—and unattached. And, if there was, his secretary wasn't in the running. And now here you are, proving them wrong. And you don't *appreciate* it. I could weep.'

'Paul isn't considerate,' Sally said, goaded.

Jane sniffed. 'He is to you. Compared with what he's like to the rest of us when you're on leave.'

'Oh.' Sally was taken aback.

She thought about it and decided that it wasn't true. Jane was probably letting her fear of Paul's quick tongue colour her reactions to his behaviour to stand-in secretaries. Or—which was more likely, she thought wryly—Jane the romantic was trying to convince them both that Paul was genuinely fond of Sally. Jane had done that before, come to think of it. Or tried to.

Sally bit her lip, looking out of the window. The idea was laughable, she told herself sensibly. Or it should have been. If only something that wasn't sensible and stubbornly refused to be quiet didn't whisper in her ear that it would be wonderful if it was true. She blinked. Jane didn't seem to notice, which was comforting. She turned back to her, schooling her face with a calm expression.

'And he's falling over himself to make it up to you because this wedding is such a rush,' Jane began and then stopped. 'The man's a dream-boat,' she finished hurriedly.

Silly tipped her head back, staying calm with an effort. 'I'm sure you're right,' she said quietly.

'So why are you so offhand with the poor guy?'

'I suppose I don't have the temperament to get excited about things the way you do,' Sally apologised, hoping it was true.

Jane was incredulous.

'Not excited about your own wedding?'

Sally's smile was twisted. 'Not the way you mean, no.'

Jane drew a long breath. 'If that's not offhand, I don't know what is,' she said roundly. 'If not downright ungrateful.'

'I'm sorry. I'm just not romantic, I suppose.'

'You're crazy. You're marrying the sexiest man in London.'

Sally was shaken by a little laugh. 'If you say so. But, believe me, Paul's not romantic either.'

Jane shook her head. But to Sally's enormous relief she let the subject drop.

They swept up to the Randolph Hotel in expensive silence more than an hour before the wedding was due to take place.

Jane marched her into the hotel with one hand under her elbow as if she were under guard, as Sally pointed out.

'Too right,' Jane said drily. She turned to the desk clerk. 'We'd better have a couple of brandies to take with us.'

The girl smiled. It was clear that she knew exactly why they were there.

'Just ring Room Service. The number's in the room. And anything else that we can do, of course, we'll be happy to. I hope you have a very happy day, Miss Harrison.'

'Thank you,' said Sally hollowly.

In the lift she said accusingly, 'You told them it was a wedding party.'

Jane shrugged. 'I may have mentioned it. What does it matter? It may even get you a bottle of free champagne.'

'Free hemlock would be more welcome,' Sally muttered.

Jane was impatient. 'Why make such a fuss? Would you rather I'd told them it was a dirty weekend?'

'It's Monday,' Sally pointed out.

Jane snorted and would have responded in kind, but the lift had come to a stop. A grinning attendant took them to their room and flung the door open with a flourish. He put the bags just inside the door, and Jane gave him a lavish tip.

'Come on. In,' she commanded as Sally hesitated. 'If you don't need a shower, I do. And I could do with a stiff drink——'

She broke off abruptly. Behind her Sally came perforce to a dead halt.

'What is it?'

'Well, that's how they found out it was a wedding,' said Jane, recovering her cool. 'Nothing to do with me, m'lud.'

Peering over her shoulder, Sally saw that the room was filled with flowers. It was not just that there was a bunch of flowers on a table. Or even two tables. They were everywhere—in huge urns, baskets, bowls. On the dressing-table and the ledge beside the bed and the floor.

Jane looked at them eloquently.

'Not romantic, huh?'

Sally picked the embossed white envelope from among an artistic swirl of leaves and lilies. She knew the black handwriting. So he hadn't just had a telephoned message inscribed by the florist.

'*Trust me.*'

Sally's eyes stung. She turned away.

'I think you're right,' she said in a careful voice. 'A brandy is what I need.'

Jane picked up the phone. 'Tension,' she said briskly. She gave the order and put the phone down. 'Feel sick?'

'A certain amount of digestive turbulence,' Sally agreed.

Jane beamed at her. 'That's the first natural thing you've said all day. At least you've got bridal nerves. Even if you've dispensed with all the other traditional emotions.'

Sally gave a weak chuckle at that. 'Sorry to disappoint you.'

Jane looked at her curiously. 'It's not me you're disappointing. Sally...'

'Yes?'

'Sally, this thing with you and Paul—it *is* all right, isn't it? I mean, you do want to marry him?'

Sally ran her finger down the scented stamens of a golden lily.

'Why do you ask?'

'Well, I know you have this image of being the coolest thing outside the polar ice cap, but... I mean, you don't seem very happy and... Oh, I don't know what I mean.' She bit her lip. 'Paul is normal enough—excited and full of plans—but you...'

It was ironic, Sally thought, listening impassively, that Jane should think she was the one who was cool and unmoved. She didn't know Paul as well as Sally did, of course. She would see the energy, the charm and enthusiasm—and mistake them for the real thing. It was easy enough to do if you weren't a practised watcher of Paul Theokaris.

'It's as if you think there's some kind of conspiracy to get you married to him,' Jane went on slowly. 'I didn't realise it until just now.'

Sally was startled. Was that really how she was behaving? She thought she'd made up her mind to agree to his bargain and live with the consequences. Was she still hoping, in her heart of hearts, that the bargain would get varied somehow? That he'd change his mind and not need to marry her any more? Or—and this was pure fairy story, she knew—suddenly discover that he had been in love with her all along?

She caught herself. Jane's pretty face was anxious.

'Don't worry about it. I'm happy to be marrying him,' she said reassuringly.

She shivered a little. She had forgotten to cross her fingers. She always did when she told downright lies. Not to have done so now felt like bad luck. And today she needed all the luck she could get. She shouldn't be taking chances.

There was a knock on the door.

'Medicinal refreshment,' said Jane, her mood changing.

She opened the door. Sally made her way round a trelliswork of ivy intertwined with freesias and roses in search of the tiny bathroom. She looked up and her eye fell on the full-length mirror that someone had thoughtfully provided. She stopped dead.

It was not the mirror that made her catch her breath, though it was a handsome antique with cherubs and trailing foliage carved on its frame. It was the reflection she saw.

All the flowers made the room look smaller than it actually was, a crowded bower for a princess out of a fairy story. And, to complete the illusion, hanging on the wardrobe behind her was the princess's dress: ivory and lace and a drift of veiling.

Suddenly Sally realised what Jane had meant by a conspiracy. She stared at the dress in something like horror.

'What is that?' she croaked.

Jane was taking a tray from the waiter. She looked over her shoulder.

'What?'

Sally spun round to face the dress, her face absolutely white.

'That.'

The waiter closed the door behind him. Jane put the tray down carefully and poured a treble brandy into a balloon glass. She pressed it firmly into Sally's nerveless hand.

'Paul didn't like the idea of your not having a proper wedding dress,' she said rapidly. 'I told him we'd seen this dream of a dress when you were trying on the other stuff. So he had me call the boutique. It'll fit.'

Sally sat down heavily on the edge of the bed. The brandy splashed. She didn't notice. She hadn't tasted it.

'Did it occur to you—to *any* of you—that I meant what I said?' she said in a voice that cracked.

She stopped, biting her lip. There was no point in shouting at Jane. She knew who was responsible for this. Clever, determined, manipulative Paul. He just decided what he wanted and then made it impossible for anyone to do anything else, she thought in mounting fury. Poor Jane wasn't his accomplice; she was his dupe, just as Sally was.

She looked round the room. He wanted the appearance of a formal wedding without the substance— so she had to take part, whether she wanted it or not. And a couple of careless words about preferring flowers to diamonds had earned her this careless, meaningless display.

Sally could hardly believe how angry she was. Angry and hurt.

Jane hesitated. 'Don't be angry,' she said tentatively. 'You'll thank him one day when you look back.'

Sally shut her eyes. 'Will I?'

Jane began to be alarmed.

'He just wants you to have a day to remember.'

Sally opened her eyes.

'Oh, I think he'll achieve that,' she said politely.

She lifted the glass and drained the spirit as if it were lemonade. Jane watched her uneasily.

'So what next? The hairdresser and the make-up artist?' Sally asked with a fierce smile.

Jane winced. 'You said you didn't want one.'

Sally was shaking.

'I said I didn't want a pantomime wedding dress too. But that didn't seem to make much difference. I thought Paul might have decided he wanted me blonde for the wedding.'

She put the glass down very carefully and put a hand to her face. It was icy cold.

Jane was plainly horrified. 'It isn't like that. This isn't just for him.'

'Isn't it? That's what it feels like.'

Jane sat down heavily on the dressing stool. She looked really disturbed.

'What *is* it with you two? Don't you ever talk to each other? He wanted you to be happy.'

Sally stood up and walked over to the dress. It hung against the wall like a limp ghost: waiting for flesh and blood to give it movement.

My flesh, she thought. My blood. To give life to an illusion. What's going to be left when he's finished with me? A wardrobe of expensive clothes and some dead flowers? Her throat tightened.

She didn't say any of it. She had already said too much to Jane, and anyway there was no point. Nobody was going to spirit her away from this dreadful wedding. It got worse by the moment, but long years of keeping her own counsel and doing what was expected of her was going to take her through it. She would smile and look composed and everyone would be pleased with Paul's thoughtfulness. And she would be the only one who knew how little he cared.

Knowing the truth always gave you an advantage. At least, it did in a battle. And this was coming more and more to look like a battle.

'Happy?' Sally echoed as if it were a word in a foreign language.

She put out a hand and touched the dress. The material was papery and cool to the touch. She withdrew her hand instinctively. Jane looked more and more troubled.

'I'd better get into it, then.'

Jane surged to her feet. 'You're talking about a beautiful dress. Not handcuffs.'

Sally shivered, then caught herself. 'Of course.' She managed a brief smile. 'I'll have that shower you were talking about, I think.'

Jane bit her lip. 'There's—something here for you. You—it was meant as a present.'

She held out a box with the name of a famous store on it. Sally took it, astonished. Inside, wrapped in swathes of crackling tissue paper, was a set of gossamer underwear. Sally had seen such garments in magazines and films, never in real life. There was a pair of sheer silver stockings as well.

Her mouth tightened as she looked at them. She had been wrong. He might not demand a blonde—but nevertheless Paul was going to turn her into something as close as he could get to the confident seductresses he was used to. She could have screamed.

She went into the bathroom, banging the door.

She stood under the thousand needles of the shower for as long as she dared. She managed to come out smiling.

She even managed to put on that temptress's satin and lace. She carefully did not think about whether, later, Paul would require to inspect his gift or even to remove it in person. She had got beyond self-consciousness for the moment but she was not sure how secure her composure might prove under pressure.

Jane sent her an anxious look. 'Feeling better?'

Sally nodded.

'Would you like me to help you?' Jane asked hesitantly, looking at the dress.

Sally swallowed. She took a deep breath and took it off its hanger. It had a long zip at the back.

'If you'd just...'

'Of course.'

She pulled it over her head, trying hard not to feel as if the delicate stuff was suffocating her.

'You don't need to hold your breath,' Jane said chattily. 'There's more room than I thought. You must have lost weight.' She zipped it up with a flourish. 'There you are. Beautiful. Now all you need is to do something about your hair. And you're ready.'

Sally's heart lurched. But her head was bent and Jane didn't see the look on her friend's face. Sally kept her head bent a good deal after that. It seemed sensible.

She had a bad moment at the door of the church. It was the chapel of Paul's old college, where he still knew people. They had arranged this rapid ceremony. As a consequence the small group gathered in the chapel were all his friends. Sally was startled by the number. She could feel all their eyes on her, as she stood there on

Gramps's arm, with her long skirts drifting in the little draughts of the medieval chapel.

She wondered how many of them knew the marriage for the sham it was. She shivered. Then she felt Gramps's hand tighten over her own where it was hooked into the crook of his arm. She looked up quickly.

For a moment her eyes dazzled, looking into the darkness of the little chapel. She was aware of the blackness of ancient wood and the ethereal jewel colours that the sun spangled over it through the stained-glass windows. The deep shadows whirled for an instant, shot through with unexpected light and drawing her inexorably to meet the eyes of the man standing in front of the altar.

He had half turned. He was looking at her gravely. It was almost a question. She could feel the intensity of his eyes beating at her like the ruby and sapphire shadows that dappled the cavernous interior. They could have been standing breast to breast instead of an aisle's length apart. Sally suddenly found it difficult to breathe.

She tore her eyes away and fixed them firmly on the ground.

But when she got to his side and he took her hand Paul pulled her round to face him. She could feel him willing her to look up. Slowly, slowly, half of her fighting it, she did so.

In the shadows, his face was very dark. There were wasp-stings of reflected light along the high cheekbones. The deep-set eyes glittered. She had the strangest feeling that he was in the grip of fierce triumph.

On command, she held out her hand submissively for his ring. He held her icy fingers as if he would bring them to life with the sheer overwhelming vitality of his own body. Sally felt as if a high wind were beating at her. She almost staggered under it. As if he felt it, Paul tightened his grip until it hurt, his eyes brilliant.

Sally steadied herself. By an effort of will, she concentrated on the words of the service. Her responses came collectedly in a cool little voice. Anyone watching her would have thought she had not a nerve in her body, she thought wryly. She was rather proud of herself. But she did not risk another look into those smouldering eyes.

There was a party afterwards.

'Don't tell me,' she said lightly to Paul as he led her towards one of the college common-rooms. 'Another surprise to spoil me.'

He gave her a sharp look. Whatever anyone else might think, Paul picked up the acid in her carefully neutral tone.

'I gather you haven't appreciated the others.' He did not sound surprised.

'Did you think I would?'

There was a pause. Then he shrugged.

'Sally, my darling, with you I never know what to think,' he drawled.

For a moment she hated him.

The party was a friendly, informal affair that slightly surprised Sally. Paul took her round, one arm possessively round her ivory silk waist, as if he was really in love and proud to be with her. It was a masterly performance. It did not endear him to her. But she took a perverse pleasure in playing up to it.

When one smiling middle-aged woman congratulated her on her dress she said sweetly, 'I'm so glad. It was Paul's idea.'

The woman, whose name was Nicola Barnes, looked startled, as well she might.

'The dress? You mean you let him *choose* it?'

Paul, unmoved, grinned. 'More than that, Nicky. I positively thrust it upon her.'

Nicky was amused. 'Good for you. No truck with superstition?'

He raised his eyebrows.

'It probably isn't a Greek superstition, but in England we think it's terribly bad luck for the bridegroom to see the wedding dress before the wedding,' Sally explained with relish.

Paul chuckled. 'I make my own luck.'

Nicky laughed aloud at that. 'You do, too. You always have. I must say, I never thought I'd see my wildest pupil a respectable businessman.'

'Occasionally respectable, Nicky,' Paul protested. 'And Sally thinks not respectable enough.' He glinted a laughing look down at Sally. 'Isn't that true, darling?'

'I haven't seen any signs of respectability,' she returned.

Nicky looked delighted. 'You're obviously made for each other,' she said. Impulsively she leaned forward and kissed Sally on the cheek.

Paul's eyes did not leave Sally's flustered face.

'Yes, that's what I think,' he said softly.

Sally choked.

They left while the party was still going strong. Sally was reluctant but Paul insisted.

'They'll go on to the small hours,' he said. 'Some of them haven't seen each other for a few years.'

Sally was surprised. 'But they all foregathered at short notice for your wedding?'

Paul laughed. 'They couldn't believe it. They came to make sure it wasn't a joke.'

She winced. Was that why he had insisted on the ceremony and the fairy-tale dress? And swamped her with lavish flowers that didn't mean a thing? To convince his friends, who knew him too well?

'Yes,' she agreed hollowly.

He sent her a swift, measuring look, which she returned with a steady smile. It was a reasonable effort, she thought. He started to speak, but she turned away.

'I won't be long.'

She changed swiftly into the clothes that she had worn that morning. Paul was waiting for her in the entrance hall of the hotel. He raised his eyebrows when he saw her.

She said quietly, 'If you wanted me to carry on dressing up you should have said.'

His mouth quirked. 'So I should,' he said equably. 'But it's all right. I wasn't planning on a ceremonial round of farewells. I wouldn't like to put any money on how much longer your temper will hold out.'

He picked up her case and took it out to the car park. Sally followed him, feeling as if she had somehow been outflanked.

The long, silent car felt familiar; one of the few familiar things in the whole unnerving day. She sat beside him and let her head fall back against the luxurious headrest. She sighed without realising it.

He glanced at her. 'Tired?'

'I didn't sleep very well,' she admitted unwarily.

He gave a soft laugh. 'That makes two of us.'

She tensed, but he said no more. He fastened his seatbelt, turned on the engine and set the car gently, skilfully out of the car park.

Sally watched him. She was almost light-headed with tension and, she realised, lack of food. The last decent meal she had had was with Paul two days ago. She didn't want to remember that occasion: not those hard hands; not the unwelcome surge of response they had unleashed in herself.

She brought herself back to the present and concentrated on the road.

They were travelling north out of Oxford. She didn't know the road and Paul didn't say where they were going. In her present, slightly dazed state, it didn't seem to matter. She sat back and watched fields and woodlands and prosperous hamlets flow past like water.

Paul drove fast but not violently. His movements were precise and efficient. She felt the car was always under his control, doing exactly what he wanted, taking the most elegant, economical course.

Sally watched the powerful hands on the wheel and had a sudden, strange sensation as he turned the wheel with a minimal urging of his palm. The long, strong fingers hardly moved but she could feel all the force in them as if they were holding her.

Suddenly her heart began to thud ferociously under her ribs. It was like a pain. She put a hand against it.

Paul sent her a quick glance. He said nothing. But the car seemed to surge forward.

Twilight was falling when they turned into a gated driveway. Sally stirred.

'Where are we?'

'Another country house. Not one on my shopping-list this time,' Paul said coolly. 'So perhaps you'll react less dramatically.'

Sally flushed and set her teeth. It was a low jibe and they both knew it. He sighed.

'That was uncalled-for. Sorry. It belongs to an old friend. You didn't seem to think much of going back to the flat for our first night together. I considered a hotel. But I thought you'd appreciate some privacy tonight.'

It was thoughtful; it was a shame it wasn't more of a success.

For one thing, the staff in the borrowed house treated them with an exaggerated discretion which embarrassed her. For another, the odd sense of light-headedness got worse and worse. She felt as if she were hovering somewhere in a corner, watching herself make uncomfortable conversation with Paul.

'I feel as if I'm not quite respectable,' Sally told him as the butler served coffee in the drawing-room and wished them a good night. She tried to laugh. 'The way they don't quite look at me. As if I've trapped you into eloping with me or something.'

Paul was lounging on the large sofa by the fire, his long legs stretched out in front of him. He had loosened his tie and he now had a lazy, relaxed, rumpled look. Sally avoided looking him. That was the only way she could think of to ignore the all too potent attraction of his laughing presence. It disconcerted her. Even though she would not look at him, she could see his face on her inner eye the moment she closed her eyes. She kept them open and concentrated on pouring coffee out of Georgian silver.

He chuckled. 'Trapped? That sounds fun. I don't think I've ever been trapped by a designing woman.'

'I'll bet you haven't,' Sally said, handing him one of the tiny coffee-cups.

He took a sip, his eyes challenging her over the rim. 'You know what I'm like about new experiences.'

'I know what you're like about winding me up,' Sally retorted. 'No dice.'

His smile grew disturbingly. But he looked mournful. 'No designs? No trap?'

She shook her head. 'Not even a tiny one.'

'Disappointing,' he murmured. 'But at least you've got over your temper.'

She thought uneasily that he didn't look disappointed. In fact, if she was asked to describe how he looked, Sally would have said that he was extremely pleased with himself.

She drank her coffee as fast as she decently could and excused herself. Slightly to her surprise, Paul did not protest. He got politely to his feet when she rose. But he did not try to touch her. He looked at her searchingly.

'May I come and say goodnight?'

Sally curbed the stab of something like panic under her breastbone and said steadily, 'Well, I'm very tired and I'll probably be asleep.'

Paul's eyes did not waver. 'I'll risk that.'

She swallowed.

'All right.' It was not very gracious or very composed, but he did not seem to mind.

He nodded. Sally hesitated, not knowing what to say. So she turned and went up to her room.

They had been given what was clearly the master suite on the first floor. Paul had a beautifully furnished dressing-room but Sally had the main room with panelled walls and family portraits. It had stopped her dead in her tracks. But she was determined not to be intimidated by the ornate over-decoration of an earlier age.

The bed was a huge antique, with a high canopy and heavy brocade curtains that Sally thought frankly claustrophobic. Struggling a little with the heavy material, she pulled them back as far as she could. Then she hauled at the equally weighty curtains across the window.

It was very black outside but at least now she could see the stars. She turned off all the lights except the small one on the bedside table, and leaned her arms on the windowsill. In the distance an owl hooted.

She did not know how long she stood there, staring out into the night. Her thoughts were in turmoil. But she was so tired that she could hardly hold on to a train of thought long enough to make a sentence. The indifferent stars seemed to mock her. The little woodland noises from the parkland outside seemed to mock her. She felt tears slide down her cheeks and knew that her last vestige of common sense had been swamped by the strangeness.

She dropped her head in her hands. She did not hear the door open.

Paul said behind her, 'Not in bed yet?'

Sally spun round. She dashed at her cheek with the back of her hand. But it was too late to hide the traces of tears. For a moment she thought his face softened.

She said not very coherently, 'It's the noises... I'm not used to the country...'

Paul strolled over to her. He came so close that she had to tip her head back to look into his face. His expression was odd, she thought, half determined, half intrigued. She had never seen him look like that before.

He said softly, 'You're as jumpy as a cat.'

'I'm tired.'

He nodded. 'A bit, maybe. But that's not all it is, is it? Or you'd be in bed and asleep by now.'

'No. I——'

He took her in his arms quite gently but without any possibility of her being able to remove herself. Sally did not even see him move. But then she was held hard against him and he was rubbing his cheek gently against her hair.

'There's no need to be scared, Sally. I promise.'

The slamming heartbeat was back, almost suffocating her.

'Let me go.'

There was a smile in his voice. 'Let yourself go.'

'This isn't fair.'

Paul sighed and held her a little away from him. He pushed her hair back with both hands and looked down into her eyes. She realised, with that distant part of her mind that still had some remnants of sense, that he looked very serious; even vulnerable.

'It's inevitable. Face it, Sally.'

'*No!*' It was almost a scream.

He sighed again. For a moment she thought he was going to let her go. Her body sagged, queerly hollow, almost in pain. Her head swam. She heard herself groan, half under her breath. She sounded like a small starving animal which had glimpsed food it knew it didn't have the strength to reach. It shocked her into immobility.

With one of his swift, unheralded movements, Paul swept her up against his chest. She could feel the rise and fall as he breathed deeply. He took her to the canopied bed and set her down, quite gently.

'Sally.'

She shook her swimming head.

The midnight hair brushed against his cheek. Paul caught his breath...

'Sally. Darling, look at me,' he said softly.

But she wouldn't.

Paul said clearly, 'I'm taking those clothes off. You can help me or not, as you choose.'

She stiffened at once, indignant. Then she saw the gleam in his eye and rapidly changed her mind. There were other better tactics to resist Paul Theokaris than a battle of the senses she was bound to lose, she thought.

So she went as limp as a rag doll. She did not actively impede him, but she fought to stay uninvolved. He got rid of her jeans, her shirt and T-shirt and then stopped as if he had been struck. She felt his hands tighten on her waist.

Unbearably tense, she opened her eyes. Paul was looking at her disbelievingly.

Sally gasped. She had forgotten the cobwebby stuff he had provided for her to wear under that princess's dress. Now, with her tumbled against the heavy brocade counterpane, it looked as if she had worn his gift deliberately. She would have felt less exposed if she'd been naked, Sally thought wildly.

Slowly his eyes travelled up her body. Her anger leaked away to be replaced by a shaming, dangerous excitement. Her muscles locked. She could have screamed under that slow scrutiny. Then, at last, his eyes met hers. His mouth quirked.

'Sally,' he said on a breath.

'No.' She tried to struggle backwards, but her limbs were like lead. She could not tear her eyes from his.

He touched her breast very gently with one finger. Involuntarily, Sally arched, her head falling back.

'Darling, you don't know what you're talking about.' Paul sounded almost sad.

She was on the rack. She said, more to herself than him, 'I—do—not—want—this.'

He took his hands away from her. Sally collapsed with a gasp as if she had been running. Her heart hurt. She stared at him.

The handsome face was a mask, the mouth a cruel line.

'No?'

Paul shook his head. He took in her slenderness in one expressive glance that swept her from head to toe. Sally felt that it left her on fire.

He wrenched off the loosened tie and flung it away from him. She remembered the look, the feel of that muscular, naked chest as she had felt it before and began to shake.

Her mouth was very dry. She tried to say 'No' again. But it would not come out right.

Paul said softly, 'Tell me to go and I will.'

The shirt followed the tie. She tried to close her eyes and could not. He came to the side of the bed and stood beside her, reaching out an imperative hand. With a sense of inevitability, she put her own into it. For the second time that day she felt her cold fingers engulfed and brought to life by his own.

Paul lifted her hand to his mouth. He bent his head. Shaken to the core, Sally felt the warmth of his tongue against the softness of her palm. She gave a soft cry and her hand turned in his; became urgent; crept round the back of his neck and, with the delight of his crisp hair under her eager fingers, pulled him down to her.

As he drifted kisses across her revealed shoulders she said, 'This isn't fair.'

Paul was sliding the straps of her underwear away. He laughed huskily.

'You are so right.'

Sally gave in to the worst temptation of her life.

'I never meant...' she began.

But Paul closed her mouth with a kiss that was unlike anything she had ever imagined; fierce and frightening and yet the height of her dreams. And his hands began to move on her in ways she had never even contemplated in dreams. From a great distance she thought he was laughing against her skin.

'I did,' Paul whispered. 'I've thought about this for a long time. There's no one like you.'

It was absolutely the wrong thing to say. It brought her down to earth with a cruel impact.

She'd counted his girlfriends once before when he was trying to resist all that practised seduction. Now, un-invited, unwanted, they paraded in front of her, every one beautiful and confident and part of his world. And every one had been in his arms, as she was now, Sally had no doubt; probably felt what she felt now. And he'd left them. As he'd leave her.

'Oh, *hell*,' she said.

CHAPTER SEVEN

PAUL'S reaction completed Sally's confusion. He leaped away from her as if he had burned himself. Then, without a word, he gathered his clothes and was gone like a shadow.

Sally came down slowly. She lay shaking among the covers, her eyes fixed on the blackness that was the door. The tension was almost unbearable. But Paul didn't come back. It was a long time before she slept.

In the morning she woke from a troubled sleep to oil-paintings of disapproving eighteenth-century figures in fuzzy landscapes. Polished floor. High ceilings. A canopied bed with silent springs. And a slowly gathering awareness of having behaved appallingly.

Sally sat up and buried her face in her hands. She was filled with a nasty mixture of guilt and regret. What had come over her last night? If Paul had thought she was ready to make love to him last night, he'd had every reason. She must have been out of her mind. How *could* she have behaved like that? If he'd refused to let her go it would have been no more than she deserved, she thought. What was she going to *say* to him?

She huddled her arms round her. There was goose-flesh on her upper arms. She realised she was naked. The implications had her hot with shame. He would be furious. She had led him on blatantly, irresponsibly. She had never felt so small.

She got up. Her clothes were tumbled all over the polished floor but she tracked them down in the end. It didn't make her feel any better.

The discreet staff were nowhere to be found. Neither was Paul. It was a relief in a way. But there was no point in putting off the inevitable confrontation. A little desperately she searched through the rooms they had used last night.

Paul was in the dressing-room. He was in bed and still sleeping. Sally stood in the doorway, hesitating. Her cheeks burned.

Paul didn't stir. He was lying on his side, turned away from her. His hair was tousled and he had pushed the covers away from him. He had an arm up, holding the pillow, which he had pulled askew under his cheek.

Cautiously Sally trod over to the bed. She looked at the naked back thus revealed. It was strongly muscled and tanned and even gold. It was beautiful, but somehow vulnerable in its nakedness. Hardly aware of what she was doing, she ran a gentle finger along his shoulder-blade in pure exploration.

Paul turned, muttering. He burrowed deeper into the pillow. Instinctively Sally smiled. Then suddenly she realised what she was doing. She flinched back, her smile dying.

She was doing it again—reaching for him, forgetting that to him she was just Sensible Sally, the convenient spouse who wasn't as much trouble as his glamorous girlfriends. And leaving herself wide open to hurt.

He turned again. This time she found herself looking into alert brown eyes. They were quite unreadable.

'Good morning,' Paul said softly.

Even in the face of that closed expression, Sally felt an unwelcome surge of longing. It filled her with embarrassment and left her shaken.

She swallowed. 'Good morning,' she said with what composure she could muster.

He shifted under the covers. Sally flinched involuntarily. With a wry expression he pulled the duvet under his arms and sat up.

At once memories flashed across her brain: of the roughness of his cheek against her breasts, his hands sweeping her limbs around and over him; his mouth. And of her own pliant, eager response. She would have given anything to dismiss them as false. But she was too honest.

She'd been rehearsing this scene since she'd woken up. Now all her careful diplomacy went out of her head.

Sally swallowed. 'I'm sorry about last night,' she said baldly.

He looked her up and down without expression. She would not be an alluring figure, she thought wryly, in her crumpled jeans, with her hair all over the place and the marks of the night's conscience on her face.

'I believe you,' he said at last.

Sally gritted her teeth. 'I shouldn't have——'

He made a weary gesture. 'No post-mortems, please.'

This was horrible. He was behaving like a polite stranger.

'I told you I wasn't comfortable... You said you'd give me time...' she found herself saying defensively.

He pushed the hair back from his face.

'Are you accusing me?' he said incredulously.

Sally flushed. 'Paul, I——'

'Look,' he said in an even tone, 'you told me to begin with that you didn't want to sleep with me yet. I accepted it. For a while last night we both thought you'd changed your mind. In the end, you hadn't. End of story.'

Sally said fiercely, 'You don't understand.'

Paul bent his head in agreement. 'You're right. I don't.'

For a moment the brown eyes weren't unreadable at all. He looked furious. Sally took a step backwards, startled.

He muttered an expletive under his breath. Then he gave an impatient sigh.

'All right. A post-mortem, if you insist.' He glared at her. 'You're free. You're adult. The chemistry's right. We're even married,' he added drily. 'What's the problem?'

Sally glared back. 'Me,' she said.

He took that with equanimity. One eyebrow flicked up. He even smiled a little.

'I wouldn't have said so,' he murmured.

Her colour rose. She looked away. 'If you mean the way I responded last night,' she said stiffly, 'I was out of my head with tiredness. I didn't know what I was doing.'

Paul laughed, 'I don't buy that. You knew perfectly well what we were both doing. Until you got cold feet.'

Sally's chin rose. 'That's not fair.'

'Have you been fair? To either of us?'

That went home. Sally felt herself flinch and knew he had seen it too. She didn't answer. She turned her head. Inside she was shaking. But outwardly she was not doing a bad job of looking composed. If, that was, you did not look at the whiteness of the knuckles, where her hands were locked together in front of her. She thought that Paul would be noticing. The laughing eyes did not miss much, for all their laziness. And at the moment he was not even laughing.

She said carefully, 'If we're talking about fairness... Let's not forget that this is a short-term contract we have here, Paul. I don't think you can expect me to behave as if it's a death-us-do-part marriage.'

'I told you we would make love,' he reminded her.

That, of course, was true. And she had thought she would be able to hide her own feelings; forget about his girlfriends and his unflatteringly practical reasons for marrying herself. Only now she was realising she wouldn't forget them till the day she died.

'Love?' She gave a harsh laugh.

Paul's eyebrows rose. 'I thought we'd had this conversation.'

Sally felt guilty again and perversely annoyed with him for making her do so.

She said defensively, 'I changed my mind.'

Paul's eyes narrowed. 'When?'

Well, at least he hadn't asked why, she thought on a rush of relief.

He sat up suddenly and reached for her, pulling her down to sit beside him on the bed. His hands were hard, almost cruel. He shook her slightly.

'When? As soon as the settlements were signed?'

She stared. His mouth took on a hard line.

'Cards on the table, Sally. You were broke. Whom would you have married if you hadn't married me?'

Sally winced. He shook her again, harder.

'I shouldn't have married anybody,' she shouted.

There was a long silence. His hands fell from her shoulders. She eased herself away from him. Paul did not try to prevent her. When she stole a look at him, his face was thoughtful.

As if he felt her eyes on him, his gaze flickered. He met her look, his expression unreadable. He set his shoulders back against the bed-head and let the anger drain visibly out of him.

'That would have been a definite waste,' he drawled.

Sally felt raw and hurt and humiliated. She could have screamed.

Paul clasped his hands behind his head and regarded her. She could not help noticing the way the dark hair fell over the long, clever fingers. Even at this moment, when she could cheerfully have strangled him, she had an urge to touch his hair, to intertwine those fingers with her own; to lean forward and kiss him.

I must be *crazy*. She dashed the back of her hand across her eyes in a quick, clumsy movement. If Paul thought she was crazy too, Sally thought wryly, she couldn't blame him.

But then he astonished her. He reached out a long, tanned arm and very gently ran the back of his forefinger down her cheek. She closed her eyes.

He sighed.

'I suppose it's my fault. My timing was lousy and I didn't read the signs right.'

He sounded annoyed with himself but only faintly. Probably he could usually rely on his experience to ensure that he did read the signs right, Sally thought, lashing herself with the reflection. With women he really wanted he wouldn't go wrong. She opened her eyes and tried to assume a calm expression. Paul met it levelly.

'All right. You want time? You shall have it. Goodness knows what it'll do for my peace of mind. But it's yours. For the moment, anyway,' he added wryly.

Sally stared at him in disbelief. Paul made an impatient sound and cupped her face with both hands.

'I want you to be happy. I want us both to be happy. I won't have you turning me into a villain,' he said.

That was so unexpected that Sally looked blank. He grinned, though it was not his usual gleam of wicked fun.

'Since it upsets you so, I won't touch you again. For as long as my resolution holds out. And yours, of course,' he added on a sudden chuckle.

Sally gasped. It would be only too easy to turn to him, even now, melted by that humour, that gentleness. She grabbed for her fast-melting resistance. He could afford to be gentle, she reminded herself, because he didn't really *care*. He even thought it was funny.

She gathered herself together and bundled off the bed, away from those too clever hands and all too perceptive eyes.

From the door she said between her teeth, 'Don't you patronise me, Paul Theokaris.'

Paul watched her. She knew the expression and she knew the quick brain was working on something he wasn't going to tell her.

He said, 'I don't think patronise is quite the word.' He looked at her levelly. He didn't seem to think this was funny, anyway, she saw with a bleak satisfaction. 'You're off the hook for the moment, Sally. I wouldn't advise you to provoke me.'

Their eyes met. It felt like a declaration of war. Sally flinched and straightened her spine.

He sat up and her heart lurched. Paul saw it, one eyebrow flicking up. She found he was laughing again.

'I'll see you downstairs in ten minutes.' It was a command.

Sally's chin went up in pure reflex. Once again their eyes clashed.

'Unless you want to stay while I get dressed,' he added gently.

Sally fled.

Breakfast was set out on a huge sideboard in the dining-room. No one was there. It made Sally uneasy and it showed. Paul was amused.

'Like the Beast's castle,' he said in thrilling accents. 'Served by invisible hands.'

She jumped and looked over her shoulder. He laughed aloud. She glared.

'Don't look so worried. I bet if you press that bell by the fireplace someone will come and give us some hot coffee,' he added, reaching for the newspaper.

He was right. Sally watched with disfavour as he made a hearty breakfast, reading her snippets from his paper. She thought, I bet he wouldn't treat Amanda Carrier like this. It made her feel distinctly disgruntled. Yet what else did she expect? she thought, annoyed with herself.

As she had already amply demonstrated, she wasn't ready for the sort of treatment he no doubt would have accorded the gorgeous Amanda, if she'd been with him. Being ignored was definitely easier to deal with. After all, she thought wryly, as his secretary, she had got used to it. And it eased the atmosphere.

For the rest of the day they were carefully friendly. Paul did not refer to their conversation of the morning. Neither did Sally. He took her for a walk in the extensive grounds, helping her over ditches and tree roots with impersonal hands. He talked about his family, too.

'They're crazy,' he said lightly. 'My grandfather was a merchant who got lucky. At least that's the official version. Personally, I suspect he was a smuggler. A self-made man, anyway. Then he married—and started behaving like the emperor of China.'

Sally stared. She was picking her way carefully among last year's pine cones, but she stopped.

'How? Cutting people's heads off?'

Paul chuckled. 'No, though I wouldn't put it past him, if he thought he could get away with it. I was thinking about his attitude to his children. He started making dynastic marriages for them.'

'Dynastic——' Sally shook her head. 'I don't believe it.'

'Believe it.' He had picked up a hazel wand and swished it at the undergrowth absently. 'Almost the first thing I can remember is the big fight about my Aunt Helen walking out on her husband. He was a very up-market Italian count.'

Sally blinked. 'The first thing you remember?'

He flashed her a smile of deep amusement.

'My grandfather had a carrying voice. And he didn't believe in the English not-in-front-of-the-children. Children were expected to take sides and join in just like everyone else.'

Sally was appalled and looked it.

'How old were you?'

He shrugged. 'Somewhere between two and three, I suppose.'

'How terrible. At least my. . .' She bit it off.

She had nearly said, 'At least my parents fought in private.' She sent him a quick look. But he was surveying the paths in front of them.

He said indifferently, 'Oh, it wasn't so bad. At least growing up wasn't a shock. I already knew.'

Sally was intrigued. 'Knew what?'

He turned and looked at her, his eyes amused.

'That life is about bargains and alliances. That people change sides. That you have to work out what you want and go for it. All good business-school stuff.'

She smiled, but she was chilled. He did not notice that either. She knew why he had married her; there was no secret about it. But it was unnerving to hear him admit that he thought all relationships were bargains like the one they had made. She bit her lip.

'This way,' Paul said.

She went. The path rapidly became too steep for conversation, which was just as well. She followed him, turning his words over and over. He sounded hard. Yet sometimes he wasn't hard. Yet might he behave kindly on those special occasions because it was part of his business-school approach to life—forming alliances, as he called it—leaving him personally unmoved?

He wasn't unmoved last night, her heart whispered.

Sally stopped as if she'd walked into a wall. No, there wasn't much doubt about last night. He had been as out of control as she. But it had been physical, she reminded herself hurriedly. Nothing emotional or spiritual there, just two people drawn to each other by magnetism of blood and bone. And most of the magnetism was felt on her side.

He was an experienced man who'd spelt out the terms of the bargain and expected her to deliver, she thought savagely. It didn't really matter to him whether she did or not in the end. Whereas to her...

Oh, lord, I've got to be careful.

He stopped at the top of the hill and put a hand down to her. She took hold of it for the last few steps. She wished she was not so conscious of the warmth of his skin or the steady beat of the pulse in the wrist under her fingers.

Unaware, it seemed, he turned away, looking with satisfaction at the vista before them. Sally put a hand to her heart and sank down on to an old wooden seat under an oak.

Paul looked over his shoulder, grinning.

'Puffed?'

It was a reasonable explanation. Sally grabbed at it. 'I'm not used to route marches after breakfast.'

'You're out of condition,' he said coolly. 'A health club. That's what you need.'

'Thank you,' she said. 'And what time do I have to go to a health club?'

His eyes glinted. 'Boss too much of a slave-driver?'

She grabbed at the lightness of tone gratefully. 'Got it in one,' she returned.

He laughed and dropped on to the seat beside her. It would have been all too easy to take her hand if he wanted to. Or even to slide his arm along the back of the seat behind her. He did neither. He clasped his hands between his knees and leaned forward to scan the landscape. Sally told herself she was not disappointed.

'You should stand up for yourself.'

The patent unfairness of this was too much for her.

'Against *you*?'

'It can be done.'

'Not,' said Sally with conviction, 'by secretaries who want to keep their jobs.'

He gave a little nod, as if she had told him something in answer to a question.

'Ah. Do you?'

She was bewildered. 'Of course. I like to pay my bills.'

'But I'm responsible for your bills now,' he reminded her softly. 'You read the trust deed very carefully, as I recall.'

'Oh.'

She remembered the painful meeting and the lawyer who had congratulated her. It had seemed ironic at the time. Now she realised: the man must have thought she had done well for herself. She was silenced.

Paul did not turn his head. He stayed looking at the horizon, a faint smile playing about the firm mouth. It was not a nice smile.

He said, 'After all, that's why you married me, isn't it?'

Sally stared at that hard, handsome profile. He was wearing his negotiating look. So he wanted something. What? Some sort of revenge for last night?

It didn't seem like the Paul she knew. But he wasn't used to being rejected, after all; especially not by his sensible, accommodating secretary. Maybe he needed to bring her to the brink of surrender to make up for having resisted him last night, she thought sourly. If so, this wasn't the way to do it. Whatever she felt for him was going to stay locked away in decent privacy where it couldn't do any harm.

'You know perfectly well why I married you,' she said crisply. 'You spelt it out for me yourself.'

The smile became detectably cynical.

'The talented brother and the needy grandparent. Sally the family sacrifice,' he mocked.

She didn't like that. It made her sound like a wimp.

'Not at all. I made a bargain just as you did.'

'How fortunate I am,' the smooth voice held a hard edge, 'that I could meet your price.'

Sally surged to her feet and swung round.

'Take that back,' she said furiously. 'Take it back at once. I won't be talked to like some tawdry gold-digger.'

Paul tipped his head back to look up at her. His eyes flickered.

'Why not? Don't like the truth, Sally?' This time the mockery was savage.

'You——' she began. And caught it back just in time. She had very nearly reminded him that it hadn't been *her* idea to marry without love. But that, she realised just in time, could take her into dangerous waters. Instead she said coolly, 'You drew up the contract, Paul. I haven't asked for anything you didn't offer right from the start.'

His eyes hardened into a diamond glitter. As he met them, her pride revolted.

'And I never will,' she flashed.

He shrugged. 'You think that now. You'll change. I've been a rich man a long time and I've driven the track before,' he said, sounding cynical. 'After all, I've bought you. You'll want your share of the price.'

Sally backed. 'You have *not* bought me. And I don't want a thing from you,' she said between her teeth.

He shrugged again. Sally's face flamed.

'I wish I'd never met you,' she raged. 'Let alone married you. If this is how you keep your bargains...'

'Oh, I keep my bargains,' Paul said softly. 'To the letter, and so will you.'

She glared at him. 'Of course.'

He searched her face. Then, with one of his disconcerting changes of mood, he smiled.

'Good.'

Sally stared at him, her thoughts in turmoil. She was suddenly sure that Paul knew something she didn't; something that gave him an advantage in whatever game he was playing. But what was the game? She wished she didn't have the feeling that there was a crucial secret that he knew and she didn't.

He was already turning away.

'Lunch,' he said cheerfully, leading the way.

Sally was preoccupied on the way back. Paul stayed pleasant, even friendly. He seemed quietly satisfied. It filled her with suspicion. She felt as if she had been playing cards with him and he had won without her even knowing the game had seriously started.

When they got back she was desperate for a breathing-space.

She said abruptly, 'I must phone home.'

His face was bland. 'No point. You'll only get the answering machine.'

Sally knew he was being deliberately obtuse.

'*My* home,' she explained sweetly.

'You're my wife. Your home is my home,' he said with equal sweetness.

She drew a breath to retort, but he went on blandly, 'If you mean your grandfather's, however, he won't be there either.'

'Won't be... What do you mean?' she said, alarmed.

'I've kidnapped him to hold hostage for your good behaviour,' Paul said, leering at her.

Her alarm dissipated. 'Don't be ridiculous,' she said calmly. 'Where is he?'

Paul laughed, relenting. 'He's in the clinic. He saw the eye specialist last week. The operation was this morning.'

'Oh,' said Sally, taken aback. She was slightly hurt. 'He didn't tell me.'

'He told me he thought you'd got enough to worry about,' Paul said drily.

'Oh,' said Sally again. She looked at him with a hint of apology. 'I didn't say...'

'That I was forcing you to marry me?' Paul asked tranquilly. He sounded quite unoffended. 'No, I didn't think you had. Your grandfather is a shrewd man.'

Sally didn't want to go into the implications of that. 'So when will he come out of hospital? And,' she added with foreboding, 'what's happening to Andrew?'

'Looking after himself for a couple of nights.' Paul was reflective. 'I got the impression he was looking forward to it.'

'I'll bet he was,' said Sally grimly.

Paul grinned. 'He's a responsible boy. And he's seeing your grandfather in hospital this evening. Jane's arranging a car.'

Sally turned the arrangements over in her mind and couldn't fault them. It made her feel oddly resentful. She didn't like the speed with which Paul had shifted the mantle of family protector on to his own shoulders. It was pleasant to have the support, of course—but did she really want things taken out of her hands quite so comprehensively?

'Very efficient,' she commented blackly. 'You must be pleased with yourself.'

Paul looked down into her mutinous face.

'If I were I'd be rapidly revising my opinion,' he said drily. 'Don't sulk, Sally.'

She glared. 'I am not sulking.'

'Yes, you are. Just because for once something takes place you haven't organised——'

'I am *not* sulking,' she interrupted furiously. 'I'm just not very keen on the way you take things out of people's hands.' She thought of his relationship with his uncle; with other members of his family. She had been sympathetic to his position in the past but now she was beginning to see things from another perspective. 'You seem to think no one can run their lives properly without you telling them what to do.'

Paul's eyebrows flew up. She thought his lips twitched. Her anger bubbled over.

'You do it at work,' she accused. 'You do it to your family. All right, you can get away with it at work because you pay them. And your family *ask* for it. But you're not doing it to my family. I won't let you.'

He took her hand. He was laughing.

'It's no good, Sally,' he said, amused. '*They* have. You will too, eventually. You'll get used to it.'

She pulled her hands away and looked straight into the laughing eyes. She got hold of her temper with an effort.

'Is that a threat?' she asked pleasantly.

He tilted his head. She saw the smile in his eyes deepen.

'A promise,' he said softly.

CHAPTER EIGHT

THE first trial of strength came immediately after lunch. Sally wanted to go to the hospital to see her grandfather. Paul wanted her to move into his flat.

'It won't take any time to move in,' she said dismissively. 'I can do it any day this week.'

'I won't be free to drive you any other day,' Paul reminded her.

She shrugged. 'I can take the train. I'm used to it.'

For some reason that annoyed him.

'Don't be ridiculous. You'll have all your stuff.'

Sally felt a pleasant sense of having scored an unexpected point.

'I can cope,' she said composedly. 'I've done it before when you needed me to stay in a hotel to work late.'

He was even more annoyed.

'My home,' said Paul between his teeth, 'is not a hotel.'

Pleased, she smiled soothingly. 'Of course not. But that's about all the personal possessions I have. One suitcase of clothes; one of books. It'll take me a couple of hours to move in. At the outside.'

Paul gave an impatient exclamation. Then he looked at her carefully and his eyes narrowed. Sally raised her eyebrows.

'Are you serious?' he said at last.

'Of course.'

His lips twitched suddenly. 'My stepmother takes more than two suitcases when she goes away for a weekend.'

Sally shrugged. 'I hate carrying suitcases.'

Unexpectedly, Paul grinned. 'So does my step-mother.' He was thoughtful. 'I don't think the women of my family have ever lifted any of their damned trunks, now you come to mention it.'

Sally digested that. She found she wasn't surprised. It was odd that such a little thing should remind her yet again how alien his lifestyle was to her own.

'I'm not going to fit in, am I?' she said slowly, almost to herself.

She was surprised at his reaction.

'Because you travel light? Don't be ridiculous,' he said, sounding annoyed again. Then, seeing her surprise, he modified his tone. 'It'll be a new experience. Another one. Stimulating.'

Sally shook her head.

'You talk as if this is a *game*,' she said, exasperated.

'It is,' said Paul. 'And——' returning to the matter in hand '——I'm moving you in tonight if you only have a knapsack. Do I make myself clear?'

Sally gave in with a shrug. Like her grandfather, she was shrewd. She recognised superior determination when she saw it, even though she didn't understand him or why he was so determined.

The fact that he got his own way so easily did not dispose her any more favourably towards him, however. She launched straight into the second trial of strength.

'Another thing,' she said belligerently. 'I'm not giving up my job.'

The laughing, clever face told her nothing.

'Did I ask you to?'

'You're starting to treat me like the little woman,' she pointed out with some justice. 'I just thought I'd make the position clear. I'm not going to sit in your flat all day arranging flowers, I give you fair warning.'

Paul looked amused. 'Is that what wives do?'

'Rich wives,' said Sally sturdily. 'And it won't do for me.'

He shrugged. 'I never thought it would.' There was a quizzical gleam in his eye. 'You know, you've got a real chip on your shoulder about rich women.'

'No, I haven't,' she snapped. 'I've got a chip on my shoulder about rich men who think they're entitled to bully everybody in sight.'

Paul chuckled. 'In that case I'm astonished you don't want to give in your notice at once.'

Sally gave him a measuring look. 'If you want me out you'll have to sack me. And I'll sue for wrongful dismissal.'

'I'm not fool enough for that,' Paul said with feeling. He looked at her wryly. 'I have a breakdown every time you go on leave. As you must know. It wasn't part of the plan to gain a wife and lose a secretary. But...'

He leaned back suddenly. He was very close, looking down into her face with an expression she could not read. She tensed, but he did not attempt to touch her.

'It's not going to be easy,' he said softly.

Sally's head reared up.

'Are you threatening me?' she demanded incredulously.

His mouth tightened. 'Of course not.'

'Then why say that?'

Paul sighed impatiently. 'Because it's true.' He sounded grim suddenly.

'I don't see why,' she began.

He stopped her with a look. 'You will,' he said. 'We'll just have to sort it out as we go along.'

She thought he added under his breath, though she couldn't be sure, 'Heaven help us both.'

*　　*　　*

He took her back to the Bromley house that evening. Andrew, home from school, was sitting at the table, uncharacteristically deep in his homework.

When Sally expressed surprise he said absently, 'The car's picking me up at six-thirty. I want to get this out of the way before I go.'

Impressed, she left him to it.

As forecast, she had only two cases. Paul stowed them in the Jaguar's boot. They looked very shabby in their luxury accommodation, Sally thought ruefully.

'Tell your grandfather we'll ring,' Paul told Andrew, ushering her out of the house.

Andrew nodded. Sally gritted her teeth over a false smile and said nothing till they were on their way. Then she turned on him.

'How dare you say I wouldn't go and see Gramps this evening?'

Paul didn't take his eyes off the road.

'I didn't. But it certainly wouldn't be sensible,' he said calmly.

'*Why?*'

'Because he'll be groggy after the anaesthetic and Andrew will be more than enough for him to cope with,' he said with great patience.

'He'll want to see me...'

'Maybe. But you're tired and upset and he's already worried about you. He needs more reason to worry as much as he needs a hole in his head,' Paul said brutally. 'Give him a break.'

Sally felt her eyes pricking. She had a nasty feeling he was right. It knocked all the fight out of her.

Paul sent her a quick look. His face softened.

'Andrew can come and have supper with us if you like,' he offered. He picked up the phone between them and held it out to her. 'Ring him and tell him.'

Sally thought of a thousand things to say—about his high-handedness; about his patronising attitude. None of them seemed adequate. In the end she took the phone and made the call.

When they got back to the London flat Sally found that Paul had been right about the interest in their marriage. The answering machine was full of calls from enquiring journalists. He flicked through the tape.

'More gossip columnists than the financial Press. I suppose that was inevitable.'

Sally snorted. Paul's appearance in the gossip columns had been mildly amusing when she was his secretary. Now she didn't like the thought of Jo cutting out snippets about herself, she found.

'What are you going to do about them?'

He shrugged. 'Nothing.' He cocked an eyebrow at her. 'Unless you'd like to give one of them an interview about how I swept you off your feet?'

Sally's look of horror answered him. He gave a shout of laughter.

'You know, you're not good for my ego,' he mused. 'To say nothing of my image. Do you think you could have a shot at a bit less dismay? I'm supposed to be settling down into a stable marriage, you know. Not setting up a fifteen-round emotional title fight.'

Sally gave him a measuring look. She was, after all, used to his teasing.

'You want me to sit on your knee in the office?' she asked sweetly.

He grinned. 'Romantic...' he murmured.

It was deliberate provocation and they both knew it.

Sally said sharply, 'You haven't a romantic bone in your body.'

Paul managed to look hurt. 'I'm the most romantic man in the world. When that's the thing of the moment.'

Caught unawares, Sally gave an inner shiver. She remembered. She also remembered her own reaction. And the speed with which he could revert to cool and laughing normality. She wished she hadn't let the conversation take that turn. She didn't want to remember those things.

She turned away and began to unpack.

'I'll take your word for it,' she said in a constricted voice.

There was a little silence. Behind her Paul opened a cupboard. Having given her a lavish bedroom of her own with a wry smile, he was exploring the hanging space.

'Ugh. Mothballs. Why on earth has the woman put mothballs in an empty cupboard?'

Sally turned round with her arms full of her wedding outfit.

'Pre-emptive strike, I suppose.'

He passed her a padded coat-hanger. The little gesture was so companionable, so domestic, that for a moment she was shaken. She made a great business of hanging up the dress.

'Does the room get used a lot?' she said through a dry throat when she had command of her voice. 'Normally, I mean?'

He shrugged. 'Not a lot. The odd friend from time to time.'

'Friend? Not family?'

Something flickered behind his eyes.

'I work with my family. I don't encourage them into my private life as well.'

He looked round again.

'It's never been anyone's special room, if that's what you're worried about. Make it your own for as long as you're here.'

He gave her a friendly smile and went out. Sally sat down hard on the corner of the bed. She felt as if he had punched her over the heart, instead of smiling in

that airy way. 'For as long as you're here.' Well, that
was clear enough. A short-term contract, soon to be dissolved. And she... And she...

And she was dangerously close to being deeply in love.
She put her hands to her cheeks.

'What have I done? What on earth have I done?'

Fortunately for the next week life was too hectic for Sally
to think about the state of her emotions.

Andrew came. He viewed the flat without interest but
he was impressed by Paul's personal computer.
Grandfather, emerging jubilantly from hospital, flung
himself with enthusiasm into interviewing the domestic
help that Paul had decided he and Andrew needed. Sally
was slightly hurt. But she had to admit she was too busy
at work to give her family the time they needed. That
included Paul, except at work.

In the flat she walked round him, carefully not
touching him or inviting his touch by word or look. She
talked to Gramps and Andrew on the telephone daily.
She fell into bed exhausted every night. Once she got
there, though, sleeping wasn't easy.

Paul was tireless. Sally wondered when he slept. He
was still at work at the computer in his den when she
bade him goodnight around midnight. And when she
brewed coffee early the next morning he was on the telephone again.

'I'd say you hadn't moved all night if you weren't
wearing a clean shirt,' she told him on the next Monday
morning.

He grinned at her over the tumbled papers.

'Complaining about my hours?'

Sally realised, startled, that she had sounded more than
a little disgruntled. She smiled reluctantly.

'I'm used to having the house to myself at this hour,'
she admitted.

His eyebrows went up. 'Competitive insomnia?'

For some reason that annoyed her.

'Don't be ridiculous,' she snapped. 'I'm just a morning person, that's all. I sleep perfectly well. And don't try and pretend that you don't. You're enjoying all this wheeling and dealing. You have quite as much sleep as you want.'

His smile was mischievous. He let the preposterous lashes droop on to his cheeks and said in a husky voice, 'How well you know me.'

Sally felt the colour rise in her cheeks, without knowing why, and was furious.

'Well enough to know when you're winding me up,' she said coolly.

Paul sighed. 'Discovered at last,' he said mournfully. The lashes lifted swiftly. He searched her face. 'You still don't really trust me, do you, Sally?' he said in quite a different voice.

She jumped.

'What makes you say that?'

Paul leaned back in his chair, stretching his shirt-sleeved arms above his head.

'You're always looking for a subtext. Hidden meanings. Hints. Evasions. You don't seem to trust me to say what I mean. It's as if you think I'm laying a trap for you.'

Sally's mouth went dry. He must have detected her careful control of her emotions this week. She tried to keep her expression cool and faintly interested but something must have given her away. Maybe her eyes flickered. Paul leaned forward suddenly, his expression arrested.

'Is *that* it? You think I've trapped you?' He sounded intrigued.

She shrugged a shoulder. 'Not seriously,' she said with an effort.

After all, once Anne Theokaris had bought the shares and the banks were lending to the company again, the trap would be open. Paul would be only too glad to say goodbye then, she thought.

His head tipped on one side. 'Interesting. Now why?' he mused, almost to himself.

Stay sensible, she told herself. Stay cool and reasonable and uninvolved—and you may get away without embarrassing Paul and yourself. Above all, keep it light.

She said carefully, 'You've always made such a point of not getting involved in office affairs. It was the whole reason I got the job working for you in the first place, if you remember—because I wasn't going to get a crush on you and start chasing, like the others.'

Paul's face was mask-like. He stood up, his hands in his pockets, his eyes veiled.

'I remember. Hoist with my own petard, you're saying.'

'No.' She stayed calm and friendly. 'No. But until the problem over the shares came up you'd never given any sign of wanting anything else.'

Paul's eyes lifted swiftly. 'Hadn't I?' he said in an odd voice. 'And if I had?'

Sally's heart lurched. But she said steadily, 'I can't imagine it.'

He took a swift step towards her, his eyes suddenly sharp. 'Try.'

She shook her head decisively, though her heart lurched again harder.

'I can't. I still can't quite believe . . .' She bit her lip and said honestly, 'That's why I feel trapped, I think. You rushed me. Once you'd talked about it, you seemed to think it was decided. And I couldn't think straight at all. All I could remember was the money . . .'

Paul said, 'Another of my own petards.' His mouth set.

Sally shrugged, though she blushed a little. 'Teenage boys come expensive. And Gramps has only got his old-age pension.'

Paul swore softly under his breath. Sally was mystified. After all, she was telling him he had made the bargain he wanted, with his commanding habit and practical outlook. Then he had won.

'So you see when you told me to marry you like that and offered me all those——'

'Added inducements,' supplied Paul without expression.

'Yes,' said Sally unhappily. 'Oh, laugh at me if you like, but it seemed like fate. As if I didn't have to make any decisions any more.'

There was a little silence.

Then, 'It must have done,' Paul said drily. 'And I walked right into it, too.'

She didn't understand that. She said with the hint of a snap, 'You walked right *over* me, you mean.' She shook her head, not very proud of herself. 'That habit of command of yours.'

He watched the changing expressions on her face.

'I knew you had misgivings,' he said at last. 'I could handle that. I didn't realise you were quite so calculating, I confess.'

In spite of the amused tone, Sally had the impression that he was very angry.

'I must say, I never expected to be married for my money.'

Definitely angry. Furious, in fact.

She raised her eyebrows. 'I don't see why. That was what you offered,' she pointed out. She took a step forward. 'We've had this conversation before and I don't like it. You're not going to make me feel guilty for doing what *you* wanted. After all, why else should I marry you? You never even pretended to be in love with me. Did you?'

Paul hesitated.

'*Did* you?'

'No,' he drawled eventually. 'We were both beautifully honest.'

'And I did the sensible thing, just as you told me,' she reminded him tartly.

'Yes,' he said slowly. 'Yes, I should have remembered that good sense of yours.' He sounded faintly bitter.

Sally hesitated. She didn't know why. Then she caught sight of the clock.

'I didn't realise it was so late,' she said, conscience stricken. 'You'll have to go.'

His mouth slanted in a mirthless smile.

'So I will,' he agreed. 'Sensible Sally.' For once the hated nickname didn't sound remotely affectionate.

He went. For no reason at all, Sally flung an unoffending ashtray at the wall. It shattered almost at once. It gave her a measure of satisfaction but she still had to fight hard to stay sensible.

At least I didn't throw myself at his feet and beg him to love me, she told herself. Or cry.

With grim determination she carried on for the next week, not dissolving into tears and begging him to make love to her. At work it was relatively easy. The office was a whirlwind of bankers, lawyers and financial commentators. It was at home that her calm demeanour cost her most.

Grandfather, on a ceremonial tour of the luxurious flat, put his finger on the problem.

'Must feel you're on show all the time,' he said surveying an elaborately framed French mirror in the hall with disfavour.

This was exactly what it felt like. But not because of eighteenth-century glass on the walls. Sally repressed a

superstitious shudder and gave him her usual calm smile.
Paul, coming out of the drawing-room to greet him,
laughed. But the dark eyes were oddly intent when they
rested on Sally. She turned away, conscious of that in-
tentness and uneasy under it.

Grandfather allowed them to take him round the flat,
poking his stick at ball and claw feet on the antique
chairs. He sniffed, announcing at last that he needed to
put his feet up. He also wanted a cup of tea.

'Real tea,' he warned Sally. 'None of your scented
muck.'

'We'll spare you the Lapsang,' Paul said, clearly much
entertained, as he guided his critical guest to a deeply
cushioned sofa and gave him a footstool. Gramps allowed himself to be made comfortable.

'That's all very well, lad,' he said.

Sally winced. Never one to beat about the bush,
Gramps went straight to the subject he had come to talk
about.

To her horror he leaned back in the chair, folded his
hands over his paunch and said, 'When are you taking
our Sally on a proper honeymoon?'

Paul's eyes danced.

'Ask Sally. I'm willing,' he murmured wickedly.

Sally caught his eyes. 'We're much too busy,' she said
repressively.

Paul turned to Gramps.

'You see, Mr Harrison?'

But Grandfather wasn't disposed to accept excuses.
'You've got some damned funny ideas,' he told Sally
roundly. He said to Paul, 'Too like her mother. Louise
was a good wife and mother, I'm not saying she wasn't.
But she never thought she ought to have any fun. In
fact,' he ended confidingly, 'she was a blasted killjoy.
Can't have Sally going the same way.'

'Thank you,' said Sally awfully.

'Scrubbing the kitchen on your wedding-day,' grumbled Grandfather, on whom the smell of antiseptic cleanliness had made a deep impression.

Paul's eyebrows rose and he sent Sally such a look of mockery that she blushed.

Grandfather didn't notice. He was pursuing his own thoughts. 'Always getting at Andrew about his room. No proper boyfriends.'

'Thank you,' echoed Paul with a chuckle, though Sally noted with a sinking heart that he had taken due note of Grandfather's unwarily offered information.

'Always said she'd never marry,' complained Grandfather. 'Now she has, she ought to be taking a proper honeymoon. No point in making a martyr of yourself to work.'

'I agree with you,' Paul assured him.

Grandfather relented. 'Not saying she didn't do well by us, the boy and me,' he allowed. He reached out and squeezed Sally's hand affectionately. 'But you've got to think of yourself and your man now. Go out and enjoy yourself while you've got the chance, Sal.'

There was something about the way he said it that made Sally wonder if he too realised that the chance wasn't likely to last long.

She went and made his tea. She brewed it strong enough to strip paint, which met with his approval, and bade him a relieved farewell when he announced he must go.

Paul took him out to the chauffeur-driven car and tucked him solicitously into the back seat. In the kitchen, Sally could hear Grandfather's protests. They sounded distinctly half-hearted.

He's like me, she thought: can't believe his luck and knows it can't last. And afraid of getting to rely on it. She scrubbed the stains left by his favourite beverage on Grandfather's cup with quite unnecessary vigour.

She heard Paul return as the car drove off. He stood in the doorway of the kitchen, watching her.

'No marriage?' he said at last, on a note of discovery. 'No marriage forever and ever? Not when Andrew left home? Not when you got too old to dash around after me or my successor? *Never*?'

After Grandfather's contribution, there was no point in trying to deny it. Sally kept her face calm and nodded briskly, quite as if it didn't matter. She thought she could almost hear the sharp brain whizzing. She tensed, trying not to let it show.

'And no boyfriends,' he pursued thoughtfully. He leaned one shoulder against the door-jamb and looked her up and down. 'I think you'd better start talking.'

She rinsed the cup and began to polish it.

In the end she said neutrally, 'It's no big deal. It just wasn't a terribly happy home, ours. Gramps didn't realise because he lived over the garage. And he thought my father was wonderful, of course.'

'Wasn't he?'

She shrugged, not answering.

'Do you know that whenever you say "my father" your voice changes?' he remarked.

Sally did know. She had been aware of it for years. Up to now no one else had seemed to notice.

She hesitated. Then, as if impelled, she went on almost angrily, 'He was very quiet. The angrier he got, the quieter he'd go. My mother used to get more and more anxious. She'd pretend she thought everything was all right and she'd talk harder and harder. I could feel him getting to boiling-point. And she wouldn't *stop*. I used to listen and pray that she'd stop. If I could feel it, why couldn't she?'

He made a move and stilled it at once.

'What did he do?' Paul said quietly.

Sally realised, faintly surprised, that she was shaking.

'He used to hit her,' she said painfully. It was almost a relief to say it. She never had before. She looked away from Paul. 'I used to know when he was going to do it. She—she was so crazy about him that she never saw it coming.' She bit her lip. 'I promised myself——' She stopped abruptly.

'You'd never get yourself in the same mess,' Paul supplied. It wasn't a question.

Reluctantly, Sally nodded.

'I see,' he said.

Some of her spirit returned. 'What do you see?' she demanded suspiciously.

'Why you could afford to marry me. Without being in love.'

Her brow creased. His smile was mocking.

'Marry for love and you risk your whole life. Marry for money and all you risk is the money,' Paul said softly. 'That's it, isn't it, Sally? And you don't care about the money.'

'You know too much,' she said involuntarily. 'Particularly about money.'

Paul gave a brief, crooked smile. 'I'd have said I knew everything there was to know. And you're teaching me my mistake every day.'

She stared at him. He sounded almost bitter. But she didn't pursue it. What was there to say? It seemed as if he wanted her to say she was in love with him and she wouldn't, she *couldn't*. Not just so he could score some point in a game she didn't understand. It was too important to her.

In the end he shrugged and went to his study.

The next morning she overslept. It had not been a good night. She took a taxi to work, as Paul had already gone. She was angry with herself—and with Paul for not waking her. He was too meticulous about not invading her room.

Today was important. It was today that he saw the bankers. Jane, she thought, would be frantic, since Costas and Paul were still barely speaking.

But Jane looked calm.

'Barnards are here,' she told Sally, pushing a notepad across the desk to her as Sally took off her coat. 'No fireworks so far.' She gave Sally a mischievous grin. 'Marriage must be mellowing him. Paul said good morning to Costas. And he positively smiled at *me*.'

'All he needed was a good woman,' Sally agreed drily.

Jane laughed and left. She patted Sally on the shoulder as she went.

'Good luck, kid.'

Sally laughed and worked her way quickly through the mountain of paper. There was a neat pile of folders awaiting Paul when the bankers left. He took the men to the lift, passing her desk without a glance.

The doors to her office banged back on their hinges as Paul flung them open with a sweeping gesture. He stood there looking at her as the doors swung behind him. His expression was grave. Sally's heart went out to him. After all his work and the sacrifice of his freedom!

'They pulled?' Sally croaked.

Paul came towards her. He put his hands either side of her waist and swung her off her astonished feet.

'They bought the whole thing,' he crowed, his expression breaking into glee. 'One look at the new capital and they were back on board. New Japanese ship. Holiday design. The lot. We'll have a new loan agreement out of them as soon as they've put it to their credit committee. And *then*,' he said, swinging her round so fast that her head began to spin, 'you and I are getting out of here.'

'Put me down,' said Sally, gasping.

Paul laughed and swirled her through another circle before he set her back on her feet.

'We've done it,' he said.

He kissed her with enthusiasm.

'Congratulations,' Sally managed. She had not returned the kiss exactly but it made her feel weak and tingling at the same time. She tried to collect her thoughts and speak efficiently. Paul ignored her efforts.

'You and I, Mrs Theokaris, are due some time away from telephones,' he told her.

'How far away?' asked Sally with misgiving.

The dark face was alight with laughter.

'Radio contact only,' Paul told her with a grin.

Sally gulped. 'You're joking,' she said without much hope.

He shook his head, eyes dancing.

'Nope.'

'But you can't just drop everything. I mean, we can't. There are things to do. People... What about the family? Paul, be serious for a moment.'

He was still laughing. 'Your grandfather told me to take you away for a proper honeymoon,' he reminded her. 'So the family expect it.'

Sally sighed in exasperation. '*Your* family. Your stepmother, for instance. All the aunts and uncles in Greece. They'll want to know about the company. Shouldn't you see them?'

Paul shrugged. 'The lawyers have told Anne all she needs to know. Costas can handle the rest.'

Sally looked at him with misgiving. 'But they're your *family*.'

A set look came over his face.

'We share some genes and an interest in an occasionally wobbly company. That's the extent of what we have in common. They don't care a straw about me, as long as I keep the dividends rolling out. And, frankly, it's reciprocated.'

Sally was silent.

His smile was crooked. 'We aren't all like you, you know, Sally. Some of us are glad to get away from home. When I left I don't know who was more relieved—me or my father or Anne.'

Sally looked at him searchingly. 'Do you hate her?'

'Anne?' Paul looked faintly astonished. 'Why on earth? Oh, the wicked-stepmother syndrome.' He laughed. 'Anne wasn't wicked. She was beautiful and greedy and not very bright. She annoyed me but she wasn't unkind to me or anything like that.'

'But you left home . . .'

'When I was a teenager. Yes. I was in full revolt. But against my father and his values. Anne was an irrelevance.'

He sounded hard. Sally wondered how much of his indifference was hard-learned.

'You married to spite her,' she said thoughtfully.

'She pushed me into a corner with her damned dramatics. That's all. Purely temporary.'

Sally flinched. The unwelcome, unaccustomed tears threatened again briefly, but she was stern with herself. She was sensible, dependable Sally and she didn't make scenes. Especially not in the office. Especially not when Paul was telling the truth, however unpalatable.

Paul must have sensed something, because she could have sworn her face didn't change. His eyes sharpened.

'I didn't mean that our marriage was temporary,' he said with great deliberation.

Sally gave him a bright smile and didn't quite meet his eyes.

'We both know the terms.'

He swore. 'Sometimes you can be so obtuse. I think it's deliberate.'

Her colour rose but she hung on to her professional composure.

'Are you going out for lunch or shall I order sandwiches?' she asked brightly.

He sent her a nasty look and picked up the folders she'd prepared.

'I've got work to do. When Japan rings, put the call straight through.'

He worked like a demon the rest of the day and Sally matched him pace for pace. By the end of it she was so tired that she could hardly stand. Paul came out of his office and looked at her unsmilingly. She was sitting behind her blank computer screen, her hands stilled on the keyboard. She had absolutely no idea what she ought to do next.

'You're beat,' he said unexpectedly.

Sally sent him a quick, surprised look.

'If you're so tired, why on earth didn't you go home?'

Sally closed her eyes briefly.

'I want to *be* home,' she explained. 'The thought of going home is ghastly. Buses and trains and people and cold winds on the streets...'

Paul gave a harsh laugh.

'I'm driving you. You haven't got to face winds or people. Get your coat.'

Like an automaton, Sally did as he told her. He guided her with an impersonal hand under her elbow. She remembered the night he had driven her home to her grandfather's. She would never have thought then that in a matter of days she would be married to him.

In one way it had been the height of her most secret dreams. Sally shivered, pulling the collar of her coat closer to her face. She had married him and lived with him for weeks that seemed like a lifetime, and he was more a stranger now than she would have imagined possible. And she was still in love with him.

He helped her into the car and got in beside her. For several minutes he said nothing. When the car was coasting gently through the watery glitter of the West End streets, he spoke.

'I meant it, you know. We're going away.'

Sally turned her head. Paul was silhouetted against the high-fashion display of a famous boutique beyond his window. He was staring straight ahead at the traffic-lights and the traffic in front. He sounded as if his mind was more than half elsewhere. He seemed very close and dark and somehow unapproachable.

'I think,' he went on in his coolest voice, 'we both need it.'

She thought of being alone with him, perhaps in that discreet manor-house again, and her heart jumped. She interlaced her fingers until they hurt.

'Where?' she asked eventually. She was proud of her calm tone.

'Greece. It's time I took my bride home,' Paul said grimly. 'And I'm not putting it off.'

And the car surged into Knightsbridge as if he was deliberately drowning her answer with his acceleration.

CHAPTER NINE

THE flight was another trial of strength. Sally sat beside a darkly silent Paul and reminded herself at ten-minute intervals that she didn't make scenes. He stayed polite—just—but every time she opened her mouth to speak he glowered.

The air hostess was attentive but faintly nervous, as if she sensed the tension between them. Sally refused champagne and smoked salmon and kept a wary eye on her uncommunicative husband.

Most of the journey he was deep in the papers he produced from his briefcase. Once he used his portable computer, frowning at the answers that came up on the little screen. Once he asked her if she would like a cup of coffee.

Neither of them referred to the savage scene they had had before they'd left for the airport.

It had been a thorough fight, with Sally standing in her bedroom door in her print pyjamas, refusing to dress. To begin with she had been quiet and reasonable in her opposition to the trip to Greece. She was too busy; she wasn't ready; Grandfather wasn't really well enough to be left... Paul had stayed implacable. She had got more agitated and, when he'd revealed that they were leaving that very morning, Sally had panicked.

She had shouted at him. Paul, reasonable at first, had ended by picking Sally up and hauling the pyjama top over her head.

'Dress,' he had said to her white, shocked expression. 'Or by heaven I'll do it for you.'

She had. But of course she hadn't had time to pack. Paul was indifferent.

He was no friendlier at Athens. He escorted her through Passport Control and Customs without speaking. He seemed hardly to notice when she skidded on the unexpectedly shiny floor. Sally set her teeth, righted herself and marched after him, hating him.

There was a car to meet them. Of course, she thought drily. This might be an impromptu and purely private visit but the head of the Theokaris empire would still expect to be treated like a king.

She said as much and got a startled look from the man stowing Paul's cases in the boot. Paul laughed harshly.

'Of course,' he agreed. 'What's the point of being the boss if you can't make people jump? After all, I made you jump often enough, didn't I, Sally, my dear? Maybe I still can.'

The unfortunate driver said hurriedly, 'It is a great pleasure to meet you, Mrs Theokaris. It is very good news that you and Paul can have a holiday after all.' He held the door open for her and said to Paul over her head, 'The boat is ready and so is the house. It was not easy, but everything is as you asked for. I hope. Rosa went over yesterday to check. She'll come back with Stefanos.'

Paul gave his first smile of the day.

'Great. But we need to pick up a couple of things first, Nick.'

'You want to go back to the house?'

'No,' said Paul and added something in Greek which made the other man laugh.

He swung in beside her and Nick got in the front and started up.

'What did you say?' Sally demanded suspiciously.

He looked down at her, his eyes glinting.

'I said we were going shopping,' he said blandly.

His temper had clearly been restored by what had no doubt been a sexist and patronising exchange with the carefully courteous Nick. Sally held on her temper and returned his look with interest.

'And that's enough to make him laugh? What a simple sense of humour you Greeks have,' she said with great sweetness.

Paul shrugged.

'OK. I said you hadn't brought any clothes with you and that you wanted to buy some even if I—thought it unnecessary.'

Sally was so angry that she didn't even blush.

'How flattering.'

'The truth is never flattery,' he told her solemnly.

She contemplated, and regretfully discarded, the idea of getting out at the next set of traffic-lights. It would have been easy enough in the slow traffic. But she had no Greek and no money and Paul had not given her passport back.

So she raised her chin and said in a cooing voice that was utterly belied by the aggressive glint in her eye, 'You'll spoil me.'

Abruptly he gave a real laugh as if his anger had been completely dispelled.

'I can try. Don't ever change, Sally.'

She was startled. But before she could think of anything to say in reply the big car swooped into a space at the side of the road.

'Just right,' said Paul. 'We'll be out in fifteen minutes. See you here.'

The driver looked dubious at the allotted interval. But he shrugged and drove off.

Paul looked after the car and murmured, 'He'll never believe it.'

Sally took it as a challenge. Used to Paul's decisive ways, she briskly selected a cotton skirt, two tops, some underwear and a pair of espadrilles on his advice. He looked at the plain cotton underwear with raised brows, plainly amused. She met his eyes. His lips twitched but he said nothing. Sally took it as a victory and realised too late that Paul had calmly added to the pile a couple of brief bikinis and a silky throw-over that was as insubstantial as a shadow.

'What are those?' she demanded uneasily. She remembered the cobwebby underwear he'd given her for her wedding and wished she hadn't.

The saleswoman took the bikinis away with his cheque.

He laughed down at her. 'You'll need some protection from the sun. Apart from me, of course,' he told her.

Sally refused to blush. She sniffed. 'The sun isn't all I'll need protection from, by the look of it,' she muttered. 'And those indecent bits of froth aren't going to provide it.'

Paul chuckled. 'We'll see.'

'We jolly well won't,' said Sally, roused. 'I've never worn anything like that in my life...'

'Then it's undoubtedly time you started.'

'...and I don't intend to start now just so you can laugh at me.'

One eyebrow flicked up. But the saleswoman was returning with his receipt, a glossy carrier-bag and an absolute entourage to escort them to the door. It took a great deal of handshaking and smiling and Greek courtesies to get them back on to the pavement as the large grey car drew up.

'See?' Paul said smugly to the driver. He ran a carelessly possessive hand over her hair and touched her cheek. 'I told you she was one in a million.'

Sally was silenced. What game was he playing? It was a game, wasn't it? Suddenly he was behaving again as he'd used to in the office before he had needed to marry and so arbitrarily picked on her.

They came to a busy marina and were swiftly embarked on a white-painted yacht. Sally could not help noticing that it was one of the largest and certainly the smartest among the forest of masts.

They were welcomed aboard by a smiling man in uniform, his friendliness not hiding his deference. Paul seemed quite unaware of it, as he was also of the luxury of the cabin furnishings or the lavishness of the meal set out for them.

Sally tried to smile and respond cheerfully to the crew's manifest interest. But nothing could have underlined more savagely the difference between her circumstances and Paul's. She felt the smile stiffen on her mouth and the champagne, on which the captain insisted, turn to ditchwater on her tongue.

Paul must have sensed it. He drew her away from the friendly officers.

'Tired?'

'A bit,' Sally said, relieved to have an excuse handed to her.

'Why don't you have a rest, then? We'll be under way in half an hour or so.'

It sounded so easy, she thought. 'We'll be under way,' said casually, as if everything ran in accordance with his whims.

'This is your boat, isn't it?' she said abruptly.

Paul's eyes narrowed. 'She belongs to the company. I've chartered her for the moment, yes.'

'For how long? Oh, as long as you want, I suppose. The boss doesn't have to commit himself to timetables, does he?' she said with a bitterness that surprised her.

Paul said evenly, 'That chip is showing again. You know exactly how the boss commits himself to timetables. I haven't had a proper vacation in two years. You know that too.' He paused. Then, his voice softening a little, he added, 'Nobody knows me as well as you do, Sally. Think about it.'

She gave a little laugh, which broke.

'Oh, I *know* you, Paul. I'm just not like you. I'm a different sort of animal altogether.'

He cast a swift glance at the officers. But they were drinking their champagne, oblivious.

'What are you trying to say, Sally?'

She made a helpless gesture.

'All this. It's worse even than London. How long do you think I'm going to be able to keep up with it?'

Paul looked exasperated. 'All *what*?'

'Private cars to meet you at the drop of a hat. Luxury yachts at your beck and call. Staff getting some secret hideaway ready for you.'

As they had obviously done before, she thought. Presumably on previous occasions for a woman Paul had *chosen* to be with, instead of an arbitrarily acquired wife.

She went on hardily, 'Retainers who *hope* everything is as you've asked . . .' Her voice was rising. She stopped and drew a steadying breath before continuing more quietly, 'Don't you see, Paul? That's where I belong. Among the retainers. I'm out of my depth with all this.'

There was a pause. Sally didn't look at him.

'Even when you're with me?' he asked softly at last.

She shook her head. 'You're the worst,' she said involuntarily.

He drew a sharp breath at that.

'*I* am? How?'

'It comes so easily to you,' she said. 'That habit of command of yours. I've told you so often. Do this, do that. Oh, you say thank you but you never really expect anyone to do anything except leap to attention.'

'I don't recall your leaping to attention much,' Paul said drily. 'I was more likely to get a lecture.'

'Oh, I leapt.'

Day after day for four years; thinking round corners so his life should be untroubled by trivia; glowing from a word of praise; breaking her heart just to keep him comfortable. Sally reviewed it all and despised herself.

'Look at how I leapt when you told me to marry you,' she pointed out.

She tried to keep it light. But she could see him register the strained note in her voice.

'Oh, I see. That was you co-operating.' Astonishingly Paul sounded amused. 'I'm glad you told me. It felt like a major campaign from where I was. And one you're never going to forgive me for winning.'

Sally turned away.

'Don't laugh at me,' she said in a suffocated voice.

'Well, someone has to. You can't carry on behaving like King Cophetua's beggarmaid,' Paul told her.

'You don't understand...' she began.

'I do.' His voice was hard. 'You've been running scared all your life. In a crisis you found the backbone to marry me. Lord knows how. Now you've got a severe case of cold feet.'

'We're completely unalike...'

'Complementary. You're a woman, I'm a man. It's supposed to be quite a good combination.'

'...and I can't just stop being me and be what you want,' she shouted.

There was another pause.

Then Paul said quietly, 'How do you know what I want?'

Sally's eyes flew to his face in astonishment. For once he didn't seem to be laughing.

'It didn't take a lot of research,' she told him, recovering. 'They were in and out of your office, remember? The Amandas and Charlottes and Gabriellas.'

'The ones you count when I'm kissing you,' Paul mused, laughing again.

She glared at him. 'That's not funny. I sent them flowers and instructed the jewellers. You can't tell me they weren't around.'

'Did you ever hear me say I wanted to marry any of them?'

Sally tossed her hair back, exasperated. This *hurt*.

'You didn't *want* to marry me. Your stepmother forced your hand. I was the least troublesome solution. Damage limitation,' she accused him.

The handsome face darkened.

'If this is untroublesome, heaven help me,' he muttered.

Sally said, 'I *told* you we shouldn't——'

'You did indeed. Was this why? Because of some nonsense about my upbringing and my expectations?'

Sally sniffed, groping for a tissue.

'It's not nonsense. You don't know what it's like—pretending all this is normal for me... I don't feel like myself any more.'

He stared at her. A muscle in the tanned cheek was twitching uncontrollably. He took her hands.

'Sally, money can't make any difference to being yourself. It buys service, I agree, but all that does is free up our time to do things we think are more important.'

'The trouble is—the most important thing for me for years has been making sure my family survive and stay together,' Sally said quietly. 'Now you've taken that away from me at a stroke. I don't have to worry any more.'

Paul frowned. 'That's a problem?'

'Yes, you stupid oaf. Of course it's a problem,' she cried, exasperated. 'Now that's gone, I—I—I don't know what's important any more. Or if anything is.'

There was another, longer pause.

'Us?' he suggested neutrally. 'Our marriage might be important, don't you think?'

'If it was a real marriage, yes,' she said with a sigh. 'Not ours. Not an arrangement for the benefit of shareholders.' She couldn't quite keep the bitterness out of her voice.

He seemed about to say something. Then he stopped. Instead his eyes swept over her like a caress. It was a shock but it was also oddly soothing. For all her wariness, her body seemed to recognise the look and respond with a languid unlocking of the senses. Suddenly everything seemed heightened: the sun on the deck, the men's voices, the gentle slap of the waves against the side of the boat; the dark intensity of Paul's eyes.

He knew it too. It was apparent from the lazy gleam in his eyes. Meeting them, Sally felt her tense nerves relax, uncurl and bask in the warmth of that look. She had never felt like that before. She felt her breathing quicken. Paul was watching her intently. A muscle beside the firm mouth twitched.

Sally felt the heat rise in her cheeks. She cast a startled look in the direction of the others and was relieved that they seemed unaware. She swallowed, keeping the smile firmly pinned to her lips. She felt dazed.

He did not touch her. The way he was looking at her mouth, he didn't need to, she thought.

'Stop worrying. Go and rest. I'll see you later,' he murmured.

She did. It was half a flight in naked panic, half something slower and deeper and altogether more out of character, Sally thought. Paul was taking her further and further away from the Sally she thought she knew.

What's he doing to me? she thought as she reached their cabin. But she was too tired to find the answers and she drifted into sleep, rocked by the movement of the sea. The last thing she remembered was a pair of dark eyes, laughing at her.

She did not know how long she slept. It felt like the first sleep she had had for weeks. She came awake to a touch on her cheek.

'We're here,' Paul said.

He was sitting on the edge of the bunk, smiling down into her sleepy eyes. He touched a finger to the vulnerable skin under her eyes and ran it gently along the line of the bone.

Sally shook her head to clear it. She came up on one elbow.

'I'll get up.'

He nodded. 'No rush.'

She opened her mouth and he flung up a hand.

'*No*. Before you say it, I haven't got the crew jumping at my slightest word. We can't get in for half an hour or so because the tide's against us.' He stood up, sending her a mocking look. 'Even my great wealth can't command the tides.'

Sally knew she was being teased. She threw a pillow at him. He caught it, laughed and withdrew.

The transfer to the island was more precarious than Sally would have dreamed. The sea stayed lively, as Paul said drily, even when the tide turned. In the end, he carried her on to the empty beach from the small rowing-boat which put them ashore, splashing through the waves that curled and leapt round his ankles.

He dropped her on to her feet on a paved path of sorts and took their bags from the grinning crew. A tall woman came towards them down the path. She was wearing a headscarf and carrying a canvas bag.

Paul grinned. 'Rosa, ready for a homeward journey. Give her a smile, darling. You'll meet again.'

And before Sally could say anything he had hoisted Rosa up into his arms, and took her out to the bobbing boat. As she passed the woman flung her a flashing smile and a greeting of unmistakable goodwill. Sally smiled back weakly.

They watched the boat return to the yacht with much waving.

'And now you're a prisoner,' Paul said cheerfully.

Sally looked at the heaving water.

'I'd say we were both prisoners,' she returned.

He gave a shout of laughter. 'Sensible Sally. How right you are.'

She winced inwardly. Would she ever be anything but Sensible Sally to him? But now was not the time to explore that. She picked up the boutique's carrier-bag and said, 'Up?'

It would have been a steep climb through the olive trees if someone hadn't cut the path. As it was, Sally stopped a couple of times, her hand to her side. Paul went up it, sure-footed as an antelope, without even catching his breath, she noted sourly.

And then they got to the house. Paul turned to look at her expression.

'Worth it?'

Sally nodded dumbly.

It was not the house itself, which was a simple crescent-shaped affair on two storeys. It was the view—pines and a rock-strewn hillside rising to a peak behind it, a great sweep of white-sanded bay below. There was not a house or another human being in sight. The path ended in steps up to a tiled terrace filled with tubs of geraniums. The walls of the house were covered with vine, intertwined with jasmine. In the early-evening air the sweetness was overpowering.

'Good,' he said.

He ran up the steps and dropped the cases on the terrace.

'Sit and look,' he said. 'It's what I always do when I get here. Everything else can wait.'

Sally followed. 'This is yours?'

Paul nodded. 'Every brick and tile.'

He had dropped on to a cushioned rattan sofa. After a little hesitation she took the armchair beside it. He raised his eyebrows but said nothing.

'I didn't know.'

'You must have heard me talk about the island.'

'Well, yes,' Sally admitted. 'But I thought it was some sort of—oh, you know...'

'I can imagine.'

There was a faint breeze off the bay. Paul turned his face into it. The dark hair rippled gently, as if invisible fingers were running through it.

Or mine, thought Sally, and felt a lurch of hunger that startled her.

He drew a long breath. Out in the bay, the sea looked silver. The waves were no more than a shimmer of light through light. The sun was sinking in a hazy apricot glow. Already the yacht looked like a child's toy as it travelled towards the horizon. The breeze was warm breath among the vines.

Sally said, marvelling, 'It's so peaceful.'

Paul turned his head. 'What did you expect?'

She made a helpless gesture. 'Not this. If I'd remembered the island I'd have thought, oh, of marinas and boats and lots of sophisticated people, I suppose.'

His mouth twisted. 'Don't tell me. A bloody great swimming-pool with sun umbrellas like something out of a vermouth advertisement. Wall-to-wall beach bunnies as well, I suppose.'

Sally smiled. 'Not quite that bad. But I confess I'd imagined more in the way of the obvious holiday luxuries. And certainly a swimming-pool.'

Paul looked eloquently at the curve of white sand below.

She laughed. 'I know. I know. But most rich men's holiday villas have a pool, admit it.'

He said softly, 'This isn't a holiday villa. This is my home.'

Sally thought she hadn't heard properly. 'I'm sorry?'

'My home,' he repeated.

She was startled by something in his voice. It moved her inexplicably. She leaned forward and put a hand on his knee.

'Tell me.'

He looked down at her hand as if it were some extraordinary artefact he'd never seen before. Embarrassed, Sally withdrew.

'No.' He took hold of it then, holding it. She could feel the warmth of his skin through the material of his jeans as if she were standing in front of a fire.

She cleared her throat. 'Were you born here?'

He gave a soft laugh. 'Oh, no. I was born on a tramp steamer in the Indian Ocean. The rebel streak is inherited.'

'Then it was your parents' home?'

'They never willingly lived together. Sometimes they stayed in the main house in Athens with my grandfather. That was why I was determined to have my own.'

'So you bought it?'

Paul chuckled. 'I built it.'

'*What?*'

'My godmother left me some money. When I inherited, I bought the land. We put the house up more or less as I could afford it. I'd go to sea for six or seven months, then come back and work on it till the money ran out.' He grinned reminiscently. 'Just about every man on the island must have worked on it over the years. It was a good time.'

Sally said curiously, 'How old were you?'

'Twenty when I started it. I ran away when I was seventeen.' He sent her a quick look. 'None of my family has ever been here.'

That sounded bleak to Sally. Paul must have seen it in her face.

'My family isn't like yours,' he said roughly. 'They wouldn't want to come here. They'd be bored. There are no shops, no nightclubs. No card games. Unless I imported all the trappings you were expecting, they'd be lost.'

'You must have been very lonely,' Sally said on a note of discovery.

He watched her, a half-smile crooking his mouth.

'I'm used to it.' But he didn't deny it.

She thought of the Amandas and the Charlottes and their escorts. He had danced and dined and played squash with them. But did he have any real friends?

She said impulsively, 'Who were you close to, Paul?'

He shrugged.

She stared. 'No one?'

'Oh, there were playmates, I suppose. No one in the sense you mean, no.'

Sally bit her lip.

He sighed, stretching his long legs in front of him. He carried her hand to his chest and held it there against his heart. She could feel the dull thunder beating under their clasped hands as if it was driving her own blood. She gave a little gasp and her fingers twisted in his. Paul took no notice.

'You must understand. When you're young and free and you hit town with money in your pocket there are always girls to go dancing with.'

He would have been devastating, Sally realised with a not wholly pleasant sense of shock. At twenty-five, tanned and fit as a runner, with his travellers' tales and that air of laughing arrogance. If he'd asked her to dance, what girl would have resisted? He wouldn't have looked at a mouse like her in those days. Inwardly she shrank, the thought a chill.

His hand tightened over hers as if he felt her withdrawal.

'You don't know what it's like—a different ship, a different town; every couple of months sometimes. You can sail with people for months, get to know them like brothers—and then there's suddenly a whole new crew. Even when you're studying, people move in and out of classes as they get ships.'

Sally tried to imagine it. He saw her face.

'It's not a bad life. You get to make your mistakes in private, anyway. And you become self-reliant. Business school was a breeze after that. So was setting up the consultancy. I can handle myself in just about any situation now.'

So that was where it came from, that commanding confidence that so intimidated her. Not, Sally realised in a flash of comprehension, from the Theokaris millions. Or even the power conferred on him by his position in the company.

It was getting dark now, the shadows advancing across the terrace. Paul gave a long sigh.

'We ought to go in and light a few lamps. And see what Rosa has left us to eat. You must be starving. You didn't have anything on the plane and you can't have had time for breakfast.'

'When you were threatening to strip me, you mean?' Sally reminded him dulcetly. 'No, I can't say I felt like egg and bacon at the time.'

Paul gave a harsh laugh, letting go her hand.

'I'm not going to apologise for that. I was in a corner and so were you. We had to do something drastic. And you were being particularly stubborn.'

Sally said curiously, 'Would you really have dressed me by force?'

He seemed to consider that. He was shaken by a laugh, the bitterness disappearing as fast as it had come.

'Eventually.'

'*Oh.*'

'Now don't start panicking again,' Paul drawled. 'It was a joke, not a statement of intent. You're the jumpiest woman I've ever met.'

He stood up and held a hand down to her.

'Come with me while I find you light and food and somewhere to rest your weary head.'

He was very tall against the darkening sky. Behind his head the first fuzzy stars were appearing. He looked like a stranger and yet she felt she had known him all her life, thought Sally. He was like one of his own Greek gods, dangerous, unpredictable, wilful—and heart-breakingly attractive. She realised, with more than a hint of alarm, that her resistance was on its last legs.

Paul drew her to her feet and held her in front of him. Only their hands were touching but Sally could feel his breath in her hair, and the beat of his blood was the same rhythm as her own now.

He took her hand and led her off the terrace into the cool interior. In the doorway, he stopped under the arch of vines and looked down at her in the shadows. He pushed her hair gently back off her face.

'Welcome,' he said very softly. 'My house is your house.'

CHAPTER TEN

SALLY stepped into the warm shadows, her hand in Paul's. Her shoes clicked on the tiles. It was the only sound apart from the thump of her heart. They were both breathing unsteadily, she realised.

Above her head Paul said softly, 'Now this is where I really start to spoil you.'

He was laughing. But there was another, deeper undertone. Sally gave a sudden sweet shiver, hidden in the darkness. His hands were light on her upper arms. But their touch sent ripples of golden feeling all through her.

'Come with me.'

He guided her through the darkened room. His hands lingered on her. But he did not tighten his hold. Sally began to tremble inwardly.

He led her up a spiral staircase. She stumbled in the dark, a little fearful of the flimsy structure. Paul steadied her.

'Here.'

It was a huge room, the length of the terrace. It was dominated by a large bed with some dark cover thrown over it. But it was not the bed or the size of the room that brought Sally up short. It was the perfume. And the flowers.

They were everywhere. It was like the hotel room before her wedding, but better. Every corner of the airy apartment seemed filled with huge vases, great urns full of trailing vines and blooms she could hardly make out in the shadows. The windows must be open, she thought, because the soft breeze was making them stir, releasing little eddies of piercingly sweet scent.

Sally drew a long breath.

'It's magic.'

'Yes,' he said.

And turned her round into his arms. He was not, Sally realised, talking about the flowers.

For a long moment he held her still, his face an intent shadow in the darkness. She saw his lips part. Without volition she felt herself melt against him, her hand going up to pull his head down to her. But he turned in her grasp so that his lips just brushed her temple.

Sally made a small, hungry sound.

Paul was shaken by a soundless laugh.

'Gently,' he whispered.

His lips travelled over the sensitive skin of her eyelids. He was hardly kissing her, just touching his mouth to the quivering pulse-points. Sally held her breath until it hurt.

He gathered her up hard against his body, and his lips travelled slowly the vulnerable length of her throat. Sally arched involuntarily and her head fell back. Her hair tumbled over the strong hands that were holding her. She felt dizzy, floating, out of control. Those sustaining hands were the only barrier between her and chaos.

'Don't let me go,' she said, voiceless.

But Paul heard.

'Never,' he vowed, a smile in his voice.

She heard the smile and thought, He knows what he's doing and I don't; this is where I get terminally out of my depth. But she was beyond doing anything about it.

She felt his mouth move on her skin. She was boneless as he lifted her, carried her. He laid her on the bed and for a moment she was alone. The small winds from the sea drifted across the pillow, bringing with them the scent of pines. She turned her head, murmuring, and he was beside her again.

But he didn't kiss her. Instead he lay beside her, propped on one elbow, his hand smoothing her hair, spreading it over the pillow like a mantle. He watched absorbedly, she saw, a faint smile curling his mouth. He looked very peaceful. After a moment her heart quietened.

'A closet romantic.' His voice was teasing. 'I knew it.'

'A practised seducer,' Sally retorted, trying not to feel the pain that was closing round her heart. 'I knew that, too.'

'Practised?' He flicked the end of her nose with his finger. 'You've got to be joking. Do you know the organisation it took to get this arranged? I've never done anything like it in my life.'

She stared. 'Never taken a woman away for a romantic interlude?'

He frowned. His hand ceased its stroking.

'My *wife*.' His tone had a distinct edge to it. 'And we're not talking about some careless fling. This is the start of the rest of our lives. At least, I hope so.'

She said slowly, 'I don't understand.'

There was a pause. Then, 'I can't blame you.' Paul was rueful. 'Everything happened too quickly. I thought I was being so damned clever. And then Anne and Costas put their heads together and time ran out on me.'

He was saying that he'd had his hand forced, Sally thought painfully. He hadn't wanted to marry her. He hadn't wanted to marry at all. But, now that he had, he was going to make the best of it. She came out of the daze of delight as memory returned and, with it, sanity. She propped herself up against the pillows, withdrawing a little so she wasn't quite touching him.

'Paul Theokaris, philosopher,' she said with a mockery aimed as much at her own fragile dreams as himself.

He went very still.

'What do you mean?'

'We're into damage limitation again, aren't we?' she said with a fair imitation of calm. She even managed to sound faintly amused, which was a triumph. 'The Theokaris speciality. That's what you did when you married me in the first place. And now you're about to embark on phase two of the salvage operation.'

Another, longer pause.

'That sounds rather—cold-blooded,' he said at last levelly.

'Oh, surely not. Just practical,' said Sally, though her heart was screaming with pain.

If only he would stop looking at her like that. As if they were truly close and she was special to him. As if he loved her.

'Practical?' He shook his head in the darkness. 'That's something I've never been around you, my darling.'

She sat upright and said sharply, 'Don't talk like that.'

'What?' he said, visibly startled.

'Stop it. Just stop it,' she said, slapping her hands palm down against the covers in a fierce movement. She shook her head. The hair he was no longer caressing swung violently about her shoulders. 'I'm not one of your Amandas or your Gabriellas. And frankly I find it insulting to be treated like them.'

There was a volcanic silence.

'And how do you know how I treat them?' Paul asked, all mild politeness.

'I don't have to know from personal experience,' she hissed. 'I've seen them come into the office and I've seen them when you've finished with them. After four years I can imagine,' Sally added with a bitterness she could not contain.

'Ah.' It was crazy but Paul sounded definitely complacent. 'Jealous.'

'I am not jealous. I . . .'

'At last, something we share.'

'. . . just don't relish being played along as if I'm a fool. *What* did you say?'

'I'm glad you feel jealous too,' he repeated obligingly. 'Jealousy is a great leveller.'

Sally sank back against the headboard. She felt as if she'd had all the breath knocked out of her.

'Who on earth . . . ? You've never been jealous in your life.'

'Oh, yes, I have,' Paul said conversationally. 'Every time you wouldn't let me drive you home. Every time you went and sat in the park and ate your sandwiches with Jane. Every time you went out on a date from the office. Every time you talked about your grandfather and Andrew. As if you had no love left for anyone else.'

There was a blank silence.

Paul said carefully, 'You know what my family is like. They don't expect affection. And yours seemed to expect—everything.' He hesitated. 'You said to me that I must have been lonely. I wasn't. At least, not until I met you. And you didn't have anything left for me.'

'I don't believe you,' Sally croaked at last.

'Why not?' he asked curiously.

She floundered. 'You—you never gave any sign. You didn't behave as if you were jealous. There wasn't anyone for you to be jealous *of*. Oh, this has to be nonsense.'

'People who knew me,' Paul said evenly, 'saw the signs.'

Sally swung round to face him. But it was now almost entirely dark. Even though he was only inches away, she could not make out his expression. She did not know whether he was wearing his negotiating face. And until she knew that, she thought, could not begin to guess whether he was sincere.

She said in frustration, 'Isn't there any light in here?'

'Why?'

'I need to *see* you.'

He was shaken by a soft laugh. 'Another thing we have in common. Although I suspect our reasons are different.'

The lazy, teasing message was unmistakable. Sally heard it and her heart began to hammer. He touched her shoulder. Without realising what she was doing, she stiffened. Paul sighed.

'You know, much as I regret to say this, I think we'd better move. Temporarily at least.' There was a smile in his voice. 'If we're going to continue this discussion sensibly, that is.'

Sally swung her legs round with alacrity. The bed was so wide that even so she had to wriggle to get to the edge. Practised seducers clearly liked plenty of room, she thought, but prudently refrained from saying so.

'Let's go outside.'

She hesitated. But he came round the bed to her and, fingers lightly linked, drew her out through french windows she had barely registered before.

She could just make out the terrace below. In the distance the sea hushed and murmured like a drowsing animal. The sun had gone completely now. The sky was a great arc of blackness, shot through with turquoise where its emptiness was pierced by stars. Sally felt the vastness like a chill along her skin. She moved closer to Paul.

He slipped an arm round her.

'You're shivering. Are you cold? Of course, you still haven't had anything to eat,' he said remorsefully.

'No,' Sally said with slight surprise. 'I'd forgotten.'

'Are you hungry? You must be. I was going to see what Rosa left. But I got side-tracked.' He was laughing. 'I didn't plan to starve you into submission, honestly.'

'You wouldn't need to,' Sally said. But she said it under her breath.

'Stay here and watch the stars,' he said. 'They have a way of restoring perspective.' The back of his hand brushed her cheek very lightly. 'I'll forage and bring us back food and wine. Relax.'

Before she could say anything he had gone. Sally's hand fell to her side. No matter how long she knew him, she would never be able to predict what he was going to do next, she thought. Maybe that unpredictability made him a good businessman. It made him a hellish uncomfortable boss. And a lover?

She shivered. She had never really thought of him before as a lover. She had loved him and yearned for him, of course. But that was from a distance. A safe distance. She hadn't actually had to risk the laughter and the passion and those disconcerting changes of tack that left her floundering with only him to hold on to.

Only Paul to hold on to. But he didn't encourage his ladies to cling, she thought. And she didn't think she would have any choice. If she gave him what he wanted she would be his forever. She shivered, thinking, If he tried to walk away I'd cling for my life.

He had reminded her that she was his wife, implying that made her special. Special enough to have a permanent place in his life?

And if he did want her permanently, could she handle it? Feeling as she did, could she take his casual comings and goings? Her heart, her whole sanity, would be at risk.

Paul reappeared. He was carrying a tray which he put down on a small ironwork table Sally had not discovered. A lighter flared. And then there was a small candle glowing in the middle of a bowl of crinkled glass.

'Come and sit.'

There were chairs, too. A pair of extendable loungers, luxuriously cushioned. Sally sat, watching him open a bottle. The mushroom-shaped cork came out with a crack like a pistol-shot, followed by a controlled hiss. Sally jumped, but Paul was unmoved.

'Champagne?' she asked, recovering.

'It's a honeymoon drink.'

'Ah.' She took the tall, beautiful glass he gave her and looked at the turbulent surface of the wine. 'This really is a honeymoon? You weren't just teasing Gramps? And me?'

'What do you think?'

'I think,' Sally said carefully, 'that I don't know what game you're playing.'

He sat down, not touching her, and raised his glass to his lips. He looked at her over the rim.

'And what game are you playing? Sensible Sally?'

Whatever she was expecting, it was not that. It caught her on the raw.

'Don't call me that.'

'Why not? It's accurate.'

She winced. His voice gentled.

'Sally, back there, just a few minutes ago, you were being honest with me. I know you were scared. But you were telling the truth and not trying to double-guess me all the time. Not trying to deal with me. Now—you're back to normal. Cool and careful and self-protective Sensible Sally again.'

He paused. She looked down at her drink, hopelessly confused.

'It's not got us very far in the past, has it?' Paul asked gently. 'Don't you think you could drop it, just while we drink our champagne and talk?'

She looked up quickly. *Was* it his negotiating face? She couldn't be sure in the flickering light of the little candle. She thought he looked serious. But she couldn't be *sure*.

'I wish I had more experience,' she said involuntarily. Paul didn't smile.

'But you've run away from it,' he pointed out. 'How could you have more experience if you're not prepared to risk anything to begin with?'

Sally stared at him. 'What do you mean?' she said breathlessly.

He looked down at the wine in his glass, swirling round and round as if he saw secrets in its depths.

'I talked to your grandfather,' he said, to her absolute astonishment. 'He was worried about you, did you know that?'

'But—but why?' gasped Sally. 'And why should he tell you?'

'Because he knew how I felt about you,' Paul said evenly. He paused.

And how was that? But she didn't ask. She was too afraid of the answer, she thought with a pang.

He gave a faint sigh.

'He said you were carrying too much responsibility. And were determined to carry it alone. No boyfriends. No fun. No lovers. I quote.'

'I don't believe you,' Sally said on pure reflex. 'You're making it up. My grandfather never wanted me to have *lovers*. He'd have been shocked rigid at the idea.'

Paul shrugged. 'Not in the plural, I agree. But he wanted there to be someone for you.'

She swallowed. That at least had the ring of truth.

She said, 'I never wanted...'

'A lover,' Paul supplied. 'I know. Dear heaven, I know. I've spent years proving it on a daily basis. And until these last weeks I never knew why.'

These last weeks? Had he seen her yearning over him in the mirror? Had he uncovered her pitiful, terrible need for his love? Sally burned all over at the thought. She drained her champagne in a gulp.

From somewhere she found the courage to ask, 'What do you mean?'

He said quietly, 'Don't you realise you've been telling me? Don't you *know*, Sally?'

'I don't know what you think you're talking about,' she said harshly. 'Do you?'

She reached out and picked up the champagne bottle. It was unexpectedly heavy and swung dangerously in her hand. Paul took it from her and replenished her glass.

'Kicking over the traces at last?' he asked, his voice amused. 'Not before time, if you ask me.'

'I didn't,' she said curtly, drinking. 'What did you mean?'

He sat back in his chair twirling the long-stemmed glass between his fingers.

'Your parents,' he said. 'More particularly your mother. "Blind with love" was your phrase, I seem to recall. And horribly unhappy because of it. You promised yourself you'd never go the same way. I quote.'

She froze.

'Think about it.'

She said in a suffocated voice, 'Don't try and psychoanalyse me, Paul Theokaris.'

He drank, watching her over the top of his glass.

'Oh, I'm no shrink. But you don't have to have any special insights to see you're scared as hell of letting yourself go.'

Sally bared her teeth at him. 'Any sensible person is scared of losing control.'

'Not that scared. Not no matter what the cost.' Paul sounded calm.

That made her angry.

'Are you saying that I am?' She finished her second glass, glaring at him defiantly. 'On what grounds?'

'Most sensible people,' he said tranquilly, 'wouldn't go into someone's arms the way you came into mine if they knew they didn't want to make love with them. It isn't safe and it isn't kind.'

She didn't know if he was talking about the night of their marriage or the crazy encounter in the company flat. Sally swallowed hard. It didn't really matter which. Either would make his point for him.

She should have known that in the end he would not let her forget the way she responded to him. He was too experienced not to read the signs; to detect her overwhelming attraction to him and her helplessness in the face of it. And too ruthless not to use it against her if he really had decided he wanted her.

Wanted her quite temporarily, Sally reminded herself savagely; along with the Amandas and Charlottes, whom he presumably wouldn't be giving up. She felt as if she were fighting for her life.

She said coldly, 'You're a very attractive man. I was carried away.'

'Up to a point,' he said. His mouth quirked. 'Until you started swearing.'

Sally flushed. She set her jaw and said woodenly, 'I remembered all those girlfriends of yours.'

And how short a time we were likely to stay together.

He tilted his head. 'I thought it must be something like that. On reflection, of course. At the time I wasn't thinking very clearly.'

Sally flinched. She put her hands to her face. She was still holding the empty champagne flute and it felt icy against her hot cheek.

'How I *could* . . .'

Paul's voice was very gentle. 'I don't think you'd have done it if you'd had any choice,' he said. 'You were responding to me the way you wanted to. The way I wanted you to. And then you panicked. Didn't you?'

Not opening her eyes, Sally nodded.

'Don't look like that. It's not the end of the world,' he said. 'Especially if I'm right and we know why.'

Sally swallowed and risked opening her eyes. He met her look. Why wasn't he angry? she thought in confusion. He had every right to be. But he looked gentle and concerned; concerned for her.

'Why?' she said through a throat that hurt.

Paul hesitated. 'Sometimes people get hurt when they're young and promise themselves never again. I wondered for a bit. But then I realised—not you. You've never been close enough to a man to get hurt, have you, Sally?'

This was dreadful. The kindness in his voice scared her. Shame ran along her nerves, making her wince and turn her head away from that gentle, dispassionate gaze. She felt naked. It was worse than if he had ranted at her. She bent her head.

'No,' she whispered.

'But you're young and lovely...'

That startled her out of her shame.

'I'm not.'

'Oh, yes, you are,' Paul said calmly. His expression was wry. 'You can pin your hair out of sight and wear navy-blue mailbags, but there's no way you can hide those legs. Or that mouth,' he added reflectively. 'It used to give me some very bad nights, that mouth.'

Sally blushed. She looked at him, fascinated. Some of the shame began to dissolve in sheer curiosity.

'Young and lovely,' he went on, 'and, left to yourself, you have all the right instincts.' The smile he gave her warmed her blood. 'So...'

'So?'

'It could have been me, of course,' he said. 'I certainly frightened you that day I took you to look at Galliards. That,' he added, 'gave me a bad night or two as well. But then the first time I'd laid serious hands on you, you weren't expecting it and you were—as carried away as I was. Weren't you?'

'I don't know how carried away you were,' Sally murmured after a pause.

'The outer reaches of the galaxy,' Paul said on a little laugh. 'I'd given up all hope of your seeing me as anything but a bad-tempered boss and there you were in my arms. I went out to dinner and sat there all evening planning the wedding. Lord knows what sort of company I was.'

'You were with Amanda Carrier,' Sally reminded him.

'Was I?' He laughed softly. 'She could have been Venus de Milo for all the notice I took of her, poor girl. Costas had been telling me the bankers were worried that a bachelor wasn't committed enough to the company. I'd been wriggling like crazy because I wasn't going to tell him the way I felt about you—and I certainly wasn't going to marry anyone else. And suddenly—it seemed as if the happy ending was in my grasp.'

'And then I spoilt it all,' Sally said sadly.

Paul came out of the chair and went down on one knee in front of her. He detached the glass from her nerveless fingers and put it down on the table behind him.

'Nothing's spoilt,' he said.

'But——'

He silenced her by touching a tender fingertip to her lower lip. Sally drew a startled breath and forgot what she was going to say.

'Listen. You told me your father used to hit your mother, even though she loved him. You even told me you were like your mother.'

Sally nodded, compressing her lips against the remembered pain.

'Oh, my love,' Paul said softly. 'For a while I thought that you were so scared that you'd only married someone you were *sure* you weren't in love with. I was wrong, I think.'

He began to caress the back of her neck under the fall of hair. It was very slow and unthreatening.

'You thought that if you loved someone you invited hurt. Very understandable.' The hypnotic hand continued its rhythmic stroking. 'But that's where *you've* been wrong.'

Sally shook her head dumbly.

'Love me,' Paul urged her in a whisper. 'Let me love you. You won't get hurt. I promise.'

Without haste or force he was drawing her towards him.

'Paul, I'm frightened,' she said in despair.

He didn't release that gentle pressure. She found him smiling down into her eyes.

'Trust me,' he told her. 'I'll take care of you. You need never be frightened again.'

He'd said that before, she remembered. That was what he'd written on the flowers he'd sent her before the wedding. She watched the firm lips form the words and thought with a sense of shock, He's telling the truth.

'I love you, Sally,' he said quietly. 'I'm in way over my head. Help me.'

She was shaking. The breeze from the ocean stirred her hair. She never wore her hair down. It was an alien touch. She felt like a stranger to herself. But Paul was looking at her as if she weren't a stranger; as if he knew her to her bones. And needed her.

Sally put tentative hands on his shoulders. He looked at her gravely. She bit her lip.

Then quickly, before she lost her nerve, she leaned forward and kissed his mouth.

At once his arms went round her and he kissed her long and achingly. It made her realise the restraint he had imposed on himself. His hands tangled in her hair, moulding her face. He was murmuring against her skin, saying things she had never thought anyone would ever say to her. She made a little sound, half-sob, half-laugh.

At last he raised his head and looked down at her. Even in the uncertain candlelight, she could see that he was blazing with triumph. It was definitely not his negotiating face.

'Not spoilt at all,' he said and got to his feet, taking her with him. 'Come to bed, my darling.'

Later, tangled in the covers, with his arms possessively round her, Sally looked sleepily round the room and said, 'Is it some Greek custom? All these flowers, I mean.'

Paul gave a soundless laugh. She could feel it shake the muscular chest on which her cheek was contentedly resting.

'No, my love. That was me trying to be romantic.'

Sally lifted her head and stared into his dancing eyes. 'What?' she said, confused.

'You may remember telling me that what you would want if I was ever to shower you with gifts were flowers. Scented flowers,' Paul reminded her. He tucked a stray curl of hair behind her ear and began to caress her jaw thoughtfully.

'*I* did?' Sally said blankly. 'When?'

'Well, actually,' Paul said with a smile in his voice, 'you were being very prim about some present I was getting Amanda Carrier, at the time.'

'Oh!' said Sally, remembering. She buried her head in his chest. 'I was jealous,' she admitted.

He kissed the top of her head. 'I know. It was very encouraging. But I still committed it to memory.' He paused. 'Do you know how difficult it is to *buy* lilac?'

Sally gasped and bounced upright, looking round her. It was true. There was a great vase of purple and white lilac in the fireplace. She looked at Paul and bit her lip.

'Good lord. I didn't even notice...'

Paul gave a great shout of laughter and pulled her back against his chest.

'Don't ever tell the people in the Athens office,' he besought her. 'I arranged it, but they've been collecting the stuff from ports and airfields for me. You've got flowers from half of Europe here.'

Awed, Sally said, 'That's the most wonderful present anyone could give me. I think you're wonderful.'

'So do I,' Paul agreed. 'It was a challenge the like of which I hope never to meet again.' He kissed her. 'But worth every anxious moment.'

She got out of bed and went from vase to vase, sniffing luxuriously. Paul locked his hands behind his head and watched her appreciatively.

'Jane told me to buy you emeralds,' he said conversationally.

Sally looked up questioningly. 'Jane?'

'Unlike you,' he mocked gently, 'she's known how I feel for a long time.'

Sally bit her lip. 'She said something of the sort once. She said I was the only secretary you were kind to. I thought she was exaggerating. Or trying to be nice. I—didn't believe her.'

'She was very helpful. At least until she got carried away. She got the wedding dress for me. I wanted you to feel it was real,' he explained.

Sally nodded. 'I can see that now.' She laughed a little shamefacedly. 'I was furious at the time.'

'You looked ferocious,' Paul agreed. 'And then, when you looked at me in the chapel, I thought: We belong together and she'll realise in a minute.'

'I think I did, in a way. I was so mixed up. But I knew I wanted you to love me more than anything in the world,' Sally said shyly. 'That was why I behaved so crazily on our wedding-night. I wanted and I didn't want . . .'

He held out a tanned arm.

'Come back to bed.'

She went.

'You've got pollen on your nose,' he said, dusting it helpfully. 'I'm afraid you rather had the cards stacked against you that night. For one thing, I was going quietly crazy for you. For another, Jane got carried away with the romance of it all. She decided to give you that glamorous underwear. I thought you'd chosen it yourself, you see. So I'm afraid I rather took it as a message. That and—other things. It wasn't until she asked me whether we'd both liked your frills that I realised.'

'Oh, no,' Sally wailed. 'Oh, how stupid. And *I* thought they came with the dress and you were making me play the part.' She took his face between her hands and kissed him remorsefully. 'My poor darling, what an idiot I was.'

'Yes,' he agreed, returning her kiss with interest. 'But you see why I thought I was being invited to make love to you. I thought you'd started to trust me.'

Sally looked away, sighing. 'I was much too close to being in love with you to trust you,' she said wryly. 'And all your talk of good sense and bargains didn't help, either.'

Paul was rueful. 'To begin with I thought that was the only way I could get you. Later—well, it rather backfired. I wanted you to deny it, I suppose. But, though you were furious when you thought I was calling you a gold-digger, you admitted that it was my money that tipped the scales in my favour.'

Sally said, 'I was trying to be sensible. It was a sort of insurance. So I wouldn't be destroyed completely when it was over...'

Paul stopped her by laying a warm palm across her lips.

'I realised that when you reacted so strongly in the office when I said the temporary power struggle was over and Anne had paid up for the shares. You went white. I even *told* you I didn't mean our marriage. But you didn't look as if you believed me. I wasn't sure whether maybe you wanted to disbelieve me.' He was shaken by a little laugh. 'I'd never felt so thoroughly confused before. As if I couldn't control anything in my life any more and it was all down to luck.'

Sally looked at him under her lashes. 'You said you made your own luck,' she reminded him.

'I did, didn't I? I suppose you'll say it serves me right for my arrogance. You kept telling me I ordered people around out of habit. And I began to wonder if I'd become so dictatorial that you hated me.' He feathered a kiss across her mouth, slowly. 'Am I a monster, Sally?' he asked huskily.

The touch was sending her pulses wild.

'No,' she said gruffly. 'You're not. You're kind and sensitive and altogether wonderful. And I love you.'

He hugged her but there was distinct speculation in the look he gave her.

'In that case...'

Instantly Sally was suspicious. She knew the way those preposterous lashes hid his eyes when he was laughing at her.

'Yes?'

'You might consider an emerald or two? I know you don't really approve, but Jane's right—they go with your eyes.'

Sally narrowed the eyes in question at him.

'I might consider it. On certain conditions.'

Paul looked uneasy. 'Conditions?'

'You've made me realise,' Sally said soulfully, 'what a romantic I am.'

He sat bolt upright.

'Now come on, Sally. You've had your romance. The flowers. The champagne. I even went down on one knee in the moonlight out there,' he added, inspired. 'Be fair. What more do you want?'

Her eyes gleamed.

'Tell me you love me.'

'Ah.' Paul expelled a long breath. 'That's easy.'

He came down to her as Sally wound an arm round his shoulders and lifted her mouth.

'Where do I start? I love you...' he said along her collarbone. 'I love you...' into the hollow at the base of her throat. 'I love you...'

So they were both laughing as they drifted again into love.

Take 4 bestselling love stories FREE

Plus get a FREE surprise gift!

Special Limited-time Offer

Mail to Harlequin Reader Service®

3010 Walden Avenue
P.O. Box 1867
Buffalo, N.Y. 14269-1867

YES! Please send me 4 free Harlequin Romance® novels and my free surprise gift. Then send me 6 brand-new novels every month, which I will receive months before they appear in bookstores. Bill me at the low price of $2.24 each plus 25¢ delivery and applicable sales tax if any*. That's the complete price and—compared to the cover prices of $2.99 each—quite a bargain! I understand that accepting the books and gift places me under no obligation ever to buy any books. I can always return a shipment and cancel at any time. Even if I never buy another book from Harlequin, the 4 free books and the surprise gift are mine to keep forever.

116 BPA AJJD

Name _____ (PLEASE PRINT)

Address _____ Apt. No. _____

City _____ State _____ Zip _____

This offer is limited to one order per household and not valid to present Harlequin Romance® subscribers.
*Terms and prices are subject to change without notice. Sales tax applicable in N.Y.

UROM-93R   ©1990 Harlequin Enterprises Limited

**Relive the romance...
Harlequin and Silhouette
are proud to present**

by Request

A program of collections of three complete novels by the most
requested authors with the most requested themes. Be sure to
look for one volume each month with three complete novels by
top name authors.

In June: **NINE MONTHS** Penny Jordan
                          Stella Cameron
                          Janice Kaiser

**Three women pregnant and alone. But a lot can
happen in nine months!**

In July: **DADDY'S
           HOME**   Kristin James
                       Naomi Horton
                       Mary Lynn Baxter

**Daddy's Home ... and his presence is long
overdue!**

In August: **FORGOTTEN
           PAST**   Barbara Kaye
                       Pamela Browning
                       Nancy Martin

**Do you dare to create a future if you've forgotten
the past?**

Available at your favorite retail outlet.

HARLEQUIN   Silhouette

THREE UNFORGETTABLE HEROINES
THREE AWARD-WINNING AUTHORS

Untamed

MAVERICK HEARTS

A unique collection of historical short stories that capture the spirit of America's last frontier.

HEATHER GRAHAM POZZESSERE—over 10 million copies of her books in print worldwide
Lonesome Rider—The story of an Eastern widow and the renegade half-breed who becomes her protector.

PATRICIA POTTER—an author whose books are consistently Waldenbooks bestsellers
Against the Wind—Two people, battered by heartache, prove that love can heal all.

JOAN JOHNSTON—award-winning Western historical author with 17 books to her credit
One Simple Wish—A woman with a past discovers that dreams really do come true.

Join us for an exciting journey West with
UNTAMED
Available in July, wherever Harlequin books are sold.

MAV93

Where do you find hot Texas nights, smooth Texas charm and dangerously sexy cowboys?

Crystal Creek

AFTER THE LIGHTS GO OUT
by Barbara Kaye

Trouble's brewin'—Texas style!

Jealousy was the last thing Scott Harris expected to feel. Especially over an employee. But one of the guests at the Hole in the Wall Dude Ranch is showing interest in his ranch manager, Valerie Drayton, and Scott doesn't like it one bit. Trouble is, Val seems determined to stick to Scott's rule—no fraternizing with the boss.

CRYSTAL CREEK reverberates with the exciting rhythm of Texas. Each story features the rugged individuals who live and love in the Lone Star State. And each one ends with the same invitation...

Y'ALL COME BACK...REAL SOON!
Don't miss AFTER THE LIGHTS GO OUT
by Barbara Kaye
Available in August wherever Harlequin books are sold.